ROMANCE

Also by Gwen Davis

NAKED IN BABYLON
SOMEONE'S IN THE KITCHEN WITH DINAH
THE WAR BABIES
SWEET WILLIAM
THE PRETENDERS
TOUCHING
KINGDOM COME
CHANGES
THE MOTHERLAND
HOW TO SURVIVE IN SUBURBIA WHEN YOUR
HEART'S IN THE HIMALAYAS
THE ARISTOCRATS
LADIES IN WAITING
MARRIAGE

ROMANCE

by

GWEN DAVIS

ARBOR HOUSE
New York

For KAY BOYLE, who stood by me.
And for WILLIAM P. McGIVERN, who
sang old railroad songs, wrote
harder than anybody, and gifted us
with his presence, but not for long
enough.

This book is more than timely;
it is needed. I publish it.

Victor Hugo,
HISTORY OF A CRIME

ACKNOWLEDGMENTS

I owe a debt of gratitude to Clement Greenberg; to the painter George d'Almeida for his clarity and humor; to the art editor David Robbins for his overview on the moderns; and to Don Fine for his feisty conviction, and unremitting good taste.

November 23, 1982
—B.H.

ONE

LOVE, LOVE OF THE kind that poets grow faint from, and faith is restored by, danced that summer like fireflies above the terraces of Saint-Tropez. Resort though it was, lighthearted, filled with gawkers, the barebreasted, the self-promoters, a terrible beauty had settled on the town unexpectedly, a seriousness of thought that optimists and philosophers might have construed as the beginnings of maturity. The summer before had borne witness to the death of two local dreams: that a poet could save an economy, and that princesses could live—if not happily ever after—at least until their looks had faded. A light cloud of sorrow hung over the port, disillusion recently learned, all the harder coming as it had to those who'd considered themselves realists. Cold facts trumpeted the finale to luxury, the end of outrageous fancies, while boutique windows offered up sweaters for seven hundred dollars. And in the midst of all

11

those chanting requiems to romance and high living, while struggling toward the best table at Pizza Romana, spun Schuyler Duncan, trailing her personal light.

The road to her villa ran windingly parallel to the two-lane highway to Ramatuelle, and beside it, on the left going southward, wine grapes grew. She could not seem to get over their being there in such profusion, only a hint of custodian in their arrangement, as though the vintner, like God, had managed to achieve detachment, putting off interference or judgment until the harvest. All the more wonder, Skye considered, the grapes being sour. "They're on the Côte d'Azur in the summertime," she noted. "What more could they want? Who could they envy?"

The road curved round and twisted, tracing the same path as the Route des Plages, the other side of the vineyards, beyond a sentry line of cypress trees. On the right, clusters of high hills, capped with lush green maritime pines, discreetly sported small hotels, and occasional villas with gated driveways. From their balconies was a postcard view of that serene portion of Mediterranean where the tip of France reaches back to scratch its own underbelly, creating a covelike sea with only occasional waves, besides those cut into the surface by the windsurfers, breasts and genitals flashing in the breeze, naked oiled bodies glistening against the bright stripes of their sails. And the yachts, of course, on their way to Le Club 55 for luncheon.

Skye Duncan's vista, however, was not of the sea. Her salon, with its great double doors and balcony, faced inland, a hint that the architect, unlike Skye, had turned his back on anything too open. Her bedroom directly overlooked the garden of the Mittris, a fact of which she was unaware until she had already signed the lease, and it was too late to find anything else. The best Europeans, those who could still afford to behave like the best Europeans, followed at close distance by those who hoped to seem like the best Europeans, had all made their way south. So there was nothing available for the season, not even a hotel room.

Skye was embarrassed by the proximity, humiliated by it. On the night she drank too much wine, and broke down and wept, she told me everything that had passed between her and Gerd Mittri, everything that had failed to pass, and how stupid he would think her when he found her right next door, looking down at him. Still, she had no choice but to stay. Knowing that he had a villa there was what had brought her to Saint-Tropez.

She had tried to make up for her ignorant folly by not going to the window too much, as if the actual not seeing him, or trying to see him, would, in some way, balance the overwhelming weight of the wish to see him again. Deprived of the actual sight of him, she did penance in advance for what she was sure he would consider her foolishness.

The whole thing seemed quite touching to me, but then I am a pushover for longing, tales of knights who hover in shadowy doorways hungering for a glimpse of their ladies. Or, as I struggle toward my own growing up, and see the world as it is, ladies who hover in shadowy doorways hungering for a glimpse of their knights, since the truth is, it is we who have stayed gallant enough to yearn. To place our dreams in someone else's pocket.

All a part of innocence, I suppose, protracted as it seemed in Skye's case, and my own. We were both the same age as Christ, and by that time, we *all* should have learned. I had made the transition to being over thirty with less grace than Schuyler had, trying to attach myself to my vanishing girlishness, although it is no longer fashionable to be girlish even when appropriate in time. Womanly was something Skye had been even when the years had slotted her a teenager, radiating a grace that surpassed breeding, the ability to put everyone instantly at their ease. Ungenerously, she did not extend the same courtesy to herself, and I often thought of telling her so. But I have been brought up never to criticize my hostess, especially when she invites you for a month to the South of France. And her skittishness, really, surfaced only where Gerd Mittri was concerned. In every other area of her life she was serene, in charge, accomplished, achieved, the kind of woman you could imagine sitting for a portrait, wearing pearls, pale hands folded in her lap, without it looking like a pose.

My mother had considered it an outstanding example of my lack of judgment that I had asked Skye to be my maid of honor, on the occasion when I should have been the loveliest woman present. But then, Corinne, as she asked me to call her, Mother being matronly, inappropriate, was not too choked up with my choice of husband, either. "Brilliant," she said to me not long ago. "You're absolutely brilliant. How come you haven't made anything of your life?" I supposed that to be a pronouncement not only on my marriage, but my career, my "station," the children I hadn't had. "I adore children," she'd said once. "As long as they're other people's."

Her raising of me, such as it was, took place near what is known as the Main Line of Philadelphia, in the Quakerly triangle between Haverford and Swarthmore, characterized by that intense wish for peace never shared by my mother, especially where her marriages were concerned. Very early in my life, I was sent off to what was to become a series of boarding schools, my tenure at each dictated by the wealth and generos-

14

ity of whatever man Corinne was joined to at the time, my father declining to contribute to what he termed her delinquency at child-rearing, by paying my tuition. I learned very quickly not to become too attached to any of my stepparents, because of how precipitously they came and went. In the same way, I was reluctant to become overly fond of my schoolmates, since I never knew during what happy excursion I would be sent for and informed that I was being transferred. So it was not until I was settled in college that I dared to make a friend, and love her, and that was Schuyler Duncan.

She was waiting for me when I arrived at the Nice airport. Knowing how difficult it usually was to find a porter, and command his loyalty, she had come armed with several bottles of wine, bread and cheese, and was picnicking on the platform with three of them when my plane arrived. They all but fell over each other in their eagerness to get to my baggage, laughing, slightly drunk, enchanted, embracing her with their eyes, saluting my health and her beauty, draining what was left in their glasses.

"I didn't understand your telegram," Skye said. "What happened to Elliott?" She had invited both of us to vacation at the villa, not knowing that both of us had become one of us, since I was hard put to write any of my friends, and that is not the kind of note you drop to the alumnae bulletin.

"We're . . ." I swallowed, "divorced," I managed, not without choking slightly. I had developed a minor vocal spasm around the word, the cause of which I understood as clearly as my doctor, bringing up in me as it did all of my childhood fears, separation and alienation, my shadowy vows under the covers never to repeat my mother's folly. That lady herself regarded my divorce not as the failure I saw it, but, rather, an achieve-

15

ment. "The brains I give you no credit for," she'd said when I left him. "The brains come directly from me. But this is the first time you've used them."

"I'm so sorry." Skye put her arm around me, as we made our way through the terminal.

"Me, too," I said, and went to clear Customs.

She had changed not a bit physically since our last year in college, where she was described in the yearbook as "the girl who looked like a statue," awe in the observation. Nothing was cold about her except the high, chiseled cheeks, the wide, lofty forehead above arching, pencil-thin eyebrows, carven, thin-bridged nose, and square sculpting of jaw. The rest of her seemed in a state of constant apology for that perfection of bone. She was always smiling, the flesh of her face in perpetual movement, her expression animated, often more than circumstances warranted. I remember catching her once, in a state of unaccustomed repose: there was about her a serenity that bordered on sadness, as though she had gazed upon the truth, and found it in Camus.

But that was on one occasion only. The rest of the time she was as positive as she was lovely, which of course some people couldn't handle. If everybody liked everybody, we wouldn't have Easter.

"Why Saint-Tropez?" I asked her as they searched through my belongings. "I thought Saint-Tropez was over." My conversational French had been dormant for years, but whenever I met Frenchmen and asked them about Saint-Tropez, they had said, as in the lyrics of a song, "Saint-Tropez, c'est fini."

"It's been over so long it's back again," she said. Her eyes, almost luminous, palest mercury, seemed to darken slightly, a shadow behind them. Even when she tried to cover up a little, not telling *exactly* a lie, some inner judgment pronounced itself, giving her away. I wondered how she had ever been able to become a success in business.

"*Rien à declarer, madame?*" said the customs man.

"*Rien,*" I said, shaking my head.

"Not even to me?" asked Skye.

She looked more compassionate than curious, so I supposed I could tell her. "Well, you know how the feminists say 'Some of us have become the men we wanted to marry'? "

"Yes?"

"Well, some of *them* have become the wives we wanted to be."

"Not Elliott!"

"I can't talk about it," I said, the words themselves an illustration, bleating as they suddenly were, as if somebody were tearing out my vocal cords.

She put her hand on my arm and squeezed it, trying to infuse me with the courage she knew women had to have in what they were given for war. "It's beautiful in Saint-Tropez," she said reassuringly. "You won't be sorry you came."

"I'm never sorry I came," I said. A bad pun, but we laughed, impressed with ourselves at being ribald, naughty, and hugged each other like little girls, which I suppose we will always be to some degree. Full of mischief. Full of gratitude when someone is kind. As if our natural portion of life's banquet was crow, and a tasty dish always comes as a surprise.

WHEN I was a little girl I wrote poetry, reams of it, striving to garner with words the attention and affection denied me. I would recite at the drop of a sentence for strangers, my mother's suitors, whoever would sit still and listen, frequently bringing tears to my own eyes with the passion I felt. My freshman year in high school, a sophomore boy I very much admired told me my poetry was immature. So I stopped writing poems. That should tell you all you need to know about me and men.

When it ended with Elliott, I fell apart inside. Doubtless I should have known, certainly suspected. But he was a wonderful lover, delicate, sensitive to my needs, corresponding as they did, as I was later to realize, to so many of his own. Having experienced enough rejection in my life—each of my fathers, I was sure, was not just leaving her, but me; my lure was clearly not even great enough to capture my own mother: when all the world spoke of a face that only a mother could love, what was so awful about mine?—I was inordinately thankful for affection. And Elliott gave me a great deal of that.

When he told me the truth, the two of us wept in each other's arms, as with the grief you experience with death, before the anger sets in. I couldn't tell Corinne the real reason the marriage was ending, that it was hardly the occasion for the congratulations she confettied on me. I knew that in spite of her contempt for him, she would find more for me, say that I was not woman enough to hold him. When the truth was, no woman would have been woman enough.

TRAVELING WESTWARD along the autoroute Skye and I didn't talk very much. Too much daylight glaring to soften the facing of truths. So we pretended to marvel at the scenery, oleander burgeoning from the center divider, the pine trees we are used to at home, nothing particularly distinguishing the road from the Pennsylvania Turnpike except for the occasional sign proclaiming *Fôrets de mimosa*. But gradually the pine trees evolved, their trunks stretching slender toward the sky, great mushroom caps of green at the tops, and we were in the land of maritime pine.

As we left the highway at Le Muy, heading south toward Sainte-Maxime, in the near distance rose charred hills, specters of the previous summer's forest fires, blackened trees cringing against the sky. To the sides of the road dead oak trees proffered branches still laden with leaves, heat frozen into perennial autumn, rust and russet, as in some awful painting of fall bought at a church bazaar. A sense of desolation pulled at me, at how completely anything living can be devastated, and by nothing so complex as betrayal.

As the road curved northeastward from Sainte-Maxime toward Saint-Tropez, we began to see the tents of *Les Campeurs Sauvages.* Skye told me they were called: The Wild Campers, an invasion of those with vans and backpacks coming for their free share of beauty and summer. Like most things, their label sounded better in French, more mysterious, a hint of danger and seduction behind it, a potential novel for Graham Greene. In close translation they looked sweaty and muscular, bands around their heads, very little on their tanned bodies as they waited in front of side-opened trailers with canopies, where vendors sold *les Hot Dogs* and *pommes frites.* Crawling as the traffic now was, with a single lane to carry the hordes pressing vacationward, you could hear an occasional snatch of language. I strained my ears, stretching for some Rabelaisian babble, poetry fruited with sex.

"Il fait chaud," said a frizzy-haired young man to a svelte brown topless creature, her breasts like the conic signals that blow the direction of the wind.

"Oui," she agreed. *"Très chaud."*

What had become of the evil flowers of Baudelaire? Did everything, exposed to sunlight, become innocent? What

19

chance had I to restore by learning depravity in a climate as clean as I was? Because that's what I had decided to do to heal myself, to leap into debauchery, to prove to my own wounded psyche that women could be as filled with shadows and secret byways as men. But what if he smelled of Gauloises, and touched with hams for hands, and spoke of the weather?

"We're almost there," Skye said. In a lot on the right vans marked *Reptiles* and *Animaux* signaled the boundaries of Luna Park, a traveling carnival complete with roller coaster and Ferris wheel. "You're going to have a good time, Tess."

"I know I will." I smiled. "If I don't, it's nobody's fault but my own."

"Or Destiny's," she said, and looked out the window with that same pale intensity I had perceived in her only once before. As if she were looking for a sign, a dispute from the universe that it wasn't just Benign Indifference out there.

THERE IS a bar in San Francisco where I lived as a married woman that is known as the Body Shop, for obvious reasons. Once, when Elliott and I were coming apart, before I understood why, I had too much to drink and went there with a friend. The cruelty, the blatancy, was so sharp it penetrated even an overload of Sazeracs and stingers. Now, as anyone who has been there knows, San Francisco fancies itself—and probably is—the most cosmopolitan city in the United States. But as those who study diplomacy can tell you, the shrewdest American is no match for even a slightly schooled European when it comes to intrigue. And the little bar I considered such a hard-nosed pickup joint was a night in a nunnery compared to Saint-Tropez.

There is a rhythm to it, a formula that was explained to me

that first afternoon by a red-haired Überleutnant named Eva, who was waiting at the top of the steps to the villa when we arrived. Undeterred by my protests of exhaustion, she had set herself up to Major Domo my first impression. I was totally unprepared for the heat of the place, the blast of tropical air, African it seemed to me, heavy with hints of Casbahs and, in spite of the nearness of the sea, deserts, which, with the presence of Eva, translated itself into Rommel.

"We will be down at the waterfront to have a drink at *Senequier* at five," she said, "You will have a good time."

"I need a nap," I protested.

"Sleep you can when you're dead"—she was wearing the briefest of khaki shorts, a white T-shirt, a leopard on it with glaring sequined eyes; on her feet were beige cowboy boots, stopping at her shapely mid-calf, as though Leni Riefenstahl had elected to follow up *Triumph of the Will* with *Red River* —"or between seven-thirty and ten, when there is nowhere you must be."

"There is nowhere I *must* be, anytime."

She looked at me as though I were a piece of California fruit in which she had found Medfly larvae. "Your first impression of Saint-Tropez must be correct. You must see it on the dock from *Senequier*. I give you time to get dressed." And she was gone, her tall, lean body whipping down the steps to her silver Lamberghini, driving it off in a swirl of gravelly dust, as mercilessly as she drove herself.

"Who is she?"

"A friend of the realtor who got me this place," Skye said, following her houseman into the living room. He lugged my bags, audibly puffing, grunting, really, the Jean Gabin of the servant set. "She means well."

"She's just obeying orders?"

21

"I admit Eva's attitude is a little off-putting. But she wants everyone to love Saint-Tropez, so it will be what it was, with all the best people coming here again."

I was familiar with the lore, of the conversion of the sleepy little fishing port into the jewel of the French Riviera, when Brigitte Bardot bought a house there at the height of her fame. Like its benefactress, the luster on the resort had faded, although of course a town never has to face the reality of sagging breasts.

"Besides," Skye said, "Eva is the key to how to have a wonderful time here. She tells you all the right places to be at what hour, and all you have to do is *not* go anyplace she says. That way you can relax."

Jean Gabin dropped my luggage in my room. For a soul-searing moment I regretted Elliott's not being there with me, it was so much his kind of place. The room looked like a honeymoon, all light and powdery and frilled, with a four-poster bed. The windows were softened with valences, and lacy overhangs. My tastes have never been as fluttery as that. Perhaps, I could not help thinking, if I had decorated with a little less plaid he might never have come out of the closet, having never gone into it. "Does that mean I can go to sleep?" I asked.

"Oh, no. Today, we have to do what she says. Your first impression of Saint-Tropez must be . . ." her accent hardened into German, "Eggsellent."

THE TABLES at *Senequier* were of triangular red-painted wood, just large enough to accommodate drinks or lavish mounds of ice cream, leaving plenty of room around and behind for red canvas director's chairs jammed wooden arm against wooden arm, all facing forward. This allowed the occupants to watch

22

the passing parade of people while pretending not to be interested. The procession began just after five, or seventeen hours, as it is called in France. Huge yachts were anchored to the front of the quay, one of them Princess Caroline's in her poignant search for privacy, berthed next to Harold Robbins'. Between the yachts and the seated patrons of the cafes ambled the young and the trendy, signaling those fashions that would shortly be reported in *Women's Wear Daily.*

The girls were all pointy-breasted and slender, browned by that day's sun, the fresh glow of heat still on them, slashes of unnecessary rouge across their cheekbones, hot lilies gilded. A pregnant woman in antique lace, threads of gold woven through the fabric hugging her belly, walked proudly by, arm in her partner's. The pace of the promenaders was erratic, as though they marched to a different drummer, one that played Bach at dockside, part of a classical quintet, chamber music augmented by percussion. Many of the passersby wore cowboy boots, and the serene expressions of those whose feet did not sweat. A girl walked by with a chandelier crystal in her ear, and smiled at me, the twinkling acknowledgment of one who said how clever I was for seeing how clever she was.

Eva sat next to us, brilliant in turquoise, the field general home on leave. Turquoise dangled from her twice-punctured earlobe, the second hole outfitted with a diamond. Turquoise and diamonds clustered on her sunbrowned fingers, turquoise banded her arms, all the way up to her elbows. Turquoise linen clung to her spare, shapely hips. The color on her nails echoed the cyclamen of her lipstick, and the drink she was sipping. When Europeans coordinate, they coordinate.

Skye was watching me, studying how absorbed I was, amused at the depth of my attention. I could feel her unexpressed laughter without even turning my head as I checked

23

the grand spectacle for male fashion. Part of my assignment to myself, since debauch was the mandate for the month, was to learn how to cruise, to check men out with that same cold eye they do us, canvassing their equipment. I would have preferred my sunglasses being darker, my eyelashes longer, like Skye's, so I could cover my boldness with a geisha fan of discretion. That's one of our problems, I suppose. Even while we struggle to toughen up, we'd like to do it from a little pink cloud. One crotch in particular caught my eye—as outstanding as any I had ever seen while pretending not to look. It bulged through body-molded jeans, impressing me even while I felt disgusted with myself for being so interested. I had a close friend in San Francisco, a man, but neuter, with a voice and manner softer than mine, with whom I frequently went to gym. One day his eyes went straight between the legs of my leotard, and I felt more violated than if I had been goosed by a trucker. It is the unexpected coarseness from the sensitive man that is most insulting. In the same way, it is the unexpected indelicacy in the feminine nature that is the true embarrassment. Still, I was riveted by his crotch.

The torso above it was slim-waisted, broad-chested. His smile flashed seductively wide, free, happy, directed at no one in particular, as though it were a tourist to that face, only passing through. Had I been at a more relaxed place in my own evolution, I would have appraised him as handsome, eager, full of life. As seemed his pants. As it was, I leaned over and said he was probably in advertising.

"It isn't real," Eva noted.

"Pardon?"

"He has a towel stuffed in there. They learned it from the ballet." She was crisp, nonjudgmental in her verdict, as though that was simply the way the world was, even if not yet reported so in Newsweek.

At that moment, an uncontrollable feeling of giddiness overcame me. I could not tell if it was because of the jet lag—my spirit being nine hours behind where my body now sat, as was a good part of my brain—or because the truth was, I was unsuited for all this. I have never even vaguely tried to be a skeptic, believing flat out in God and happy endings and that somebody will keep the bomb from going off. It was Elliott who always peppered our omelets with cynical observations, trying to tell me that things are seldom what they seem, not mentioning himself as an example.

So right in the midst of *l'heure apéritive*, I let out a sob— a shock of recognition, I suppose it was—because I didn't belong there, and certainly not without him, the one who could set me straight, so to speak, on everything. The handsome young man with the maybe towel in his jeans looked over at me, and there was in his dark eyes an expression of deep surprise and pity, as if he understood how powerful an emotion had to be to show it sincerely, and at *Senequier* in the afternoon.

"Come," Skye said, and her voice was around me like a protecting blanket. "We'll go home."

THERE IS in tears, apparently, a chemical which, when retained by the body, causes hypertension, and so, down the line, stress disease, according to those who believe in holistic medicine. That is, the inner knives that tear at our bodies are sharpened by the psychic agonies we feel. Because women were, traditionally, the ones who cried, they released that chemical through their tear ducts, probably one of the reasons why they suffered less from heart diseases and strokes than men. But for every convenience, there's an equal and opposite inconvenience, as exemplified by the pain in the ass it is to empty a dishwasher. For the benefits accruing from our so-called liberation, we have to sacrifice a few disadvantaged blessings: no more tears, branding us wimps.

So for all intents and purposes, I thought I had given up crying. From the moment I faced Elliott in that lawyer's office, and the lawyer told me that he, *too*, was gay—apparently everyone wanted their cards on the table, in this case all Queens—I decided that someone in the saga had to be the hero. John Wayne lifting a fallen standard, I slipped into steadfastness like boots, ambling into the sorry sunset, as fraught with courage as Elliott suddenly showed himself fearful, my backbone seemingly forged from steel. Except for that night in the Body Shop, I hadn't cried.

But now, among the pale peach frills of Skye's guest room, her consoling voice wrapped around me, telling me to go ahead, get it all out, the disappointment and shock just flooded out of me. "I'm so humiliated," I managed to say. "I thought I was handling it so well."

"Grief isn't something you're supposed to handle," Skye said, and went to the window. Standing behind the curtain, stepping into shadow, a streak of dying afternoon sun gilding the satiny chestnut of her hair, she looked down at the garden of the Mittris. The regal coolness of her face crumbled, like a fortune cookie with no encouraging message inside. "Anyway, it could have been worse."

"How?"

"He could have left you for another woman."

26

Her name, as readers of society columns and aspirants to the circle of Truman Capote know, was Charlotte Windeler Halsey. She had met Mittri at the party which opened his showing at the Sidney Janis gallery, where she bought eight of his paintings. Skye had not wanted to be conspicuous in her admiration of him, although they had been lovers since her senior year, so she never bought more than one painting of his at a time. Her wealth, like her beauty, was something she went to great pains never to lord over anybody, especially a man so much a man of the people as Gerd Mittri. Socialists and revolutionaries hung from every limb of his family tree. His mother was the child of Marxists, fleeing Germany when she saw where Hitler was taking the philosophy of socialism; his father had been a guerrilla in the Spanish Civil War. Uncles had married daughters of the IRA, and there was a reputed cousinry to Pierre Mendès-France, which might have made him a Jew, no one was ever quite sure. Mittri's young adult life, after the university scholarships to Cambridge (England and Massachusetts), had been, in an academic way, anointed: he had taught in the art departments of two of America's finest colleges, including ours, before grants from the Ford Foundation and Guggenheim made it possible to concentrate on his own gifts.

On a less lofty level, he was sustained by Skye, who cooked for him, washed his shirts and ironed them, declining to send them out to the laundry, lavishing on his garments an almost sexual attention. At least it seemed sexual to me, so much loving concentration did she give to every inch of each seam, she who had never had to do anything for herself but tie her own shoelaces, and that with the beaming approval of a nanny. I remember seeing her dark hair shining, all of a piece, as she

27

leaned over the ironing board and talked of their plans to go to Rome, where he was to study at the American Academy.

They were living together at the time in an airy apartment on Manhattan's Sutton Place South. Or at least, she was living there, and he'd consented to sleep there and hang up his clothes. But his canvases, paints, brushes, all accoutrements of his art he kept in a loft downtown, and his papers and books he stored in a small apartment on Riverside Drive, within arguing distance of Murray Kempton and the rest of the New York intellectuals. Sometimes he took her to their parties, as though her beauty would be bright enough to blind them to the breeding she bore like a scarlet letter, branding her the child of Republicans.

He let her choose his clothes, and find the barber. And however grudgingly he agreed to let her help mold him, the configuration itself was admirable. It was reassuring to see such a smart man so smartly put together, wearing the right thing, in the right place at the right time, with the right *bon mot.* Sometimes, though, his mots were less than bon: for an industrious man he sometimes slipped lazily into insult. He equated too-quick words with quick intelligence, and in his mastery of English, his sixth language, confused the unfeeling with the urbane, as though he had drunk the milk of human kindness at the teat of George Sanders. But he was indisputably a charmer when he chose to be, which, when combined with his talent and productivity, elevated him nearly to the level of the Sistine Chapel ceiling. And, as he was one of the few living artists that one could imagine having the stamina and discipline to approximate that marvel, that was exactly where society considered he belonged.

It was Skye who had dragged him, protesting, into the right circles, as she had introduced him to the right clothes. I re-

28

member graduation weekend, all six feet four of his assistant professorial dignity slouching in seersucker, as if she had managed to transform him, with a kiss, from a frog to a Princetonian. He looked awkward, and unaccustomedly ill at ease, with none of the assurance he displayed teaching history of art. She guided him with loving, subtly manipulative hands through garden parties and teas, so that by Sunday afternoon, and the end of all the ceremonies, he seemed as relaxed as her parents were uncomfortable.

They had gifted Skye, for her graduation, with a white convertible, and a trip to Paris, where she planned to take a cordon bleu course, the better to cook for him. My parents had saved up for that occasion to tell me they were once again divorcing, the most recent spouse each had taken, as in some twentieth-century gavotte where partners who hold hands the longest are presumed not to understand the dance. Filled with my own insecurities and woes—I preferred my current mother to the original—I was not equipped to deal with the general air of excitement and celebration. Nor was I particularly interested in anybody else's happiness, not even Skye's, beloved friend though she was. Cloaked in my own dark mantle of self-pity, I chanced to pass the open convertible in which she sat with Gerd Mittri. The look of ardor on her face, the glow of love, radiated such warmth it touched even me.

I was to puzzle, of course, in subsequent years at her actions, why she degraded herself in the way she seemed to, so menially tending to his laundry, so devotionally preparing his crème brûlée. To me it seemed a kind of contrition for the privilege she had been handed, and he had been denied. Love that conquered all, or, in this case, agreed to surrender to anything, as if by its own abjectness it could raise the beloved to Alexander.

But to a college girl, which category was ending just that day, her passion was no mystery. Riddled as we were with our Brontëan dreams, it was quite all right, prescription almost, for the object of our desires to be brooding. Clearly he was brilliant, handsome, tall as already noted, with shoulders unnaturally broad, as though he held several worlds on his shoulders, which, in view of later revelations, might have been the case. Golden hair framed his head like a disorderly halo; ringlets abounded. His face was an impressive face, especially if your concept of God was Jehovah, an angry God, full of wrath. His skin was already scored with a number of deep lines, at thirty-seven, which seemed ancient then, in comparison to our twenty-two.

I suppose that artists suffer more visibly than do the rest of us. When I was still a poet, my eyes were frequently red from the pain I was able to unleash in myself, at eleven, so I suppose had I not been driven from that path, the agony would have been cumulative, and shown on my face. Not surprising then that Gerd's visage looked a little tortured. I remember one comment of his on Botticelli, where he put forth the thesis of that painter that perfection—and therefore beauty—was of a higher world, unassailable by ordinary mortals. Traditional humanists, alienated by that idea, turned on Botticelli; disgruntled and embittered, he'd given up painting and died in poverty. There was a caustic crust to that observation, as if Mittri took personally what had happened to that painter, and expected the same fate to unfold for him. At the same time he considered us part of that vast gallery of unbelievers, who could never care enough about art even while we studied it.

"The fascination with the 'Primavera' of Botticelli," it says in my notes, "is proof that men can recognize and be drawn to beauty without necessarily understanding it." I am sure that the same can be said of sex. As clever as we thought we were as undergraduates, as giddily tripping through the garden of Eros, equipped with pills and fragrant foams, we grasped no subtleties. We were greenhorns landing at Ellis Island, carnal immigrants, strangers to cunnilingus and the sly practitioners of the art of making women come.

So we imagined, if we paused to wonder, infidels that we weren't, that it was Skye's earlobe and her fingertips he was nibbling on, and that was why Skye could hardly keep her eyes and her hands off him. And not that he was bringing her to orgasm in his office between classes, that they held hurried conferences in the basement of the administration building, and would secrete themselves in the closet where the fuse boxes were, while the bell was ringing, and he would go down on her. No wonder she had such high color.

At any rate, they seemed in love on graduation day, and it cheered me for *her* future, at least. Why do we always assume that people are going to try and make each other happy? I mean, why do I?

TWO

WHEN I OPENED MY eyes, Skye was standing over me, a shade darker than she had been when I closed them, and it was night outside. It took me a moment to remember where I was, that I was in Saint-Tropez, and I wasn't married anymore. It was a little grief that pulled at my throat, as in a terrible dream when you think someone's died, and then wake up relieved because it was only a dream, and then realize it wasn't.

"How do you feel?" she asked me.

"What time is it?"

"Nine-fifteen." She was wearing white silk, bare on one bronzed, well-defined shoulder, a bright red Indian scarf with gold threads through it knotted around her slender waist. On her feet were red satin slippers, inset with gold around their delicate soles. "You slept around the clock."

She opened the window then. A flood of music came into

the room with the night air, heavy with the scent of linden trees. "The people next door are having a party."

"How come you weren't invited?" My second biggest fear in life, after being abandoned, is that I might miss something, an anxiety that surfaced when I was fourteen and realized I had not been asked to Truman Capote's Black and White Ball. That I did not know Truman Capote, that I owned nothing black and white, all seemed beside the point. Everyone worth knowing was there, which meant that I would go through my life without ever having met them, appropriate, since I myself was not worth knowing, or I would have been there.

"They don't know I'm here," Skye said. "That is, they undoubtedly know someone's rented the villa, but they don't know it's me."

"How is that possible? I would have thought everybody here would run into each other."

"I've been careful to avoid them," she said. "I want the meeting to be perfect."

"Why?" I sat up on the bed. "Who lives there?"

"Mittri," she murmured. Troilus, she might have said, so much longing, so much classical magic clung to the way she uttered his name, fairy dust sparkling around the sound of it. Her voice closed over the syllables, as though she would swallow them, and that way, at least, make him a part of her forever. "Gerd Mittri." Suddenly, there was a hard edge to her tone. "And Charlotte Windeler Halsey Mittri."

ONCE THE original discomfiture was dealt with, and Skye had resigned herself to their being next door, like a good field general who finds himself too close to the enemy, she used her vantage point to make a study of their habits. She knew what hours they went out to dine. Those few nights she left the villa, she went out early, meticulously shunning places they might turn up, the better restaurants, as Michelin-Guided by Eva. Skye never worried about running into him at *Senequier.* As long as there was daylight, Gerd would be painting. It was a mode of behavior she had marked since their days in Rome. He would leave their apartment early every morning, spend the day at the Academy, and in his studio painting, never returning until well after dusk. Even on the side trip they had taken to Venice, supposedly a lover's holiday, he had crept from their bedchamber like Romeo, with the daylight, and gone to paint. It was an orthodoxy that had become a part of his nature, past discipline, past habit, as though light itself existed for the furtherance of art, and only with darkness could he transform himself back into a human being.

From her villa window Skye could see the globular white concrete studio with its angled skylight that Charlotte had had built for him, set into the side of the hill. The Da Vinci bunker, Skye called it. He always went in just after eight in the morning, and never came out before six.

Keeping her vigil, waiting for the right time to set in motion their encounter, she usually ate at home, simple meals she cooked for herself, or Pan Bagnats she would buy from the local *traiteur,* salade niçoise on round, crisp rolls with light, mustardy dressings, cucumber adding to their crunch. I would have considered it a waste of the weeks of summer that had passed so far to be leading a life of near self-denial at Saint-Tropez were it not for how healthy she looked, and how good those sandwiches were. Rapunzel on a picnic, confining herself to the tower, till he told her to let down her hair.

She had no worries about running into Gerd that first night we went out together, once I had recovered from my pro-

35

tracted swoon. He was hosting a party, so there was no likelihood of his turning up in town. I had watched a little of the purported festivities from the terrace, and it looked to me a curiously joyless gathering, in spite of the frenzy with which the orchestra played even quiet songs. They were stationed next to the pool, in which floated rafts of white flowers with candles at their centers. The patio was strung with little white lights, flickering on and off at irregular intervals, a syncopated effect that seemed not quite perfected. There was a portable dance floor, on which only one person danced, a man in black tie, drunk I presume he was, or filled with fancy, whirling his invisible companion, dipping her deep into the steps of vanished days. The women wore long dresses, and seemed to be awaiting some signal that the party had, indeed, started. They seemed older, staid, slightly bent in their posture, as though being rich were more burdensome than people thought.

I could not see their faces, but I imagined that their smiles were fixed. The soft waves of conversation that washed up the sides of the hill to Skye's villa felt labored, spiritless, part of no unstoppable tide. It is my feeling that most parties are fiascos, putting people on edge, pressing them to be lively and attractive, when in fact they would be infinitely more lively and attractive in the company of one or two friends for whom they did not need to be lively and attractive. If I had my world, I would eliminate parties, with the possible exception of Irving "Swifty" Lazar's Oscar party, but only if I were invited.

There was one couple halfway up the hill, separate from the rest of the party, younger they must have been, making love as they were in a clump of bushes just below the ledge. They appeared as spiritless in their activity as the rest of the guests were in theirs. The boy seemed distracted as he pumped dutifully, as though it were something he had to get out of the way

36

before he was allowed to go on to what gave him real pleasure. The woman had her legs spread wide, and I could see the white of her inner thigh, in between his labored plungings, like the lights flashing staccato down below.

Skye pulled me away from my overlook, having marked what I was observing, not disapproving exactly, just noting it as a not very good example of what I'd decided to study. She murmured something about not wanting Gerd to see me. As if he would distinguish what was up there in the darkness—her terrace was unlit, the better to allow her to watch him—and would recognize, out of all the faces that had swum before him in his teaching career, mine, remembering instantly that I was her friend, and put it all together.

Just as we went inside, a burst of laughter cascaded upward, startling the night. It was what the magazines might characterize as girlish laughter, announcing to the evening that one person, at least, was spontaneous and terribly entertained, full of life, or, at least, courting it. But I could hear tightness behind the laugh, something slightly past the edge, unhinged, as though Mrs. Rochester had been loosed from her turret and thrust into ballet slippers in the South of France a few feet ahead of the rumor that she was mad.

"That's Charlotte," Skye murmured, whisking me off.

I did not share with her at the time my feeling that the possessor of that laugh sounded crazy. I suppose now, thinking back on what happened, that I might have added a measure of pity or kindness to the strange events that took place that summer, had I made my intuition known. But we are only concerned, I'm afraid, with helping the ones we love get past obstacles. It never seems to occur to us that the obstacles themselves may be in pain.

We dined that night at La Renaissance, or, as it says in

friendlier fashion on the side of the burgundy canopy, Chez Dédée, one of a number of open-air restaurants siding the Place des Lices, the town's principal plaza—a choice dictated partially by the fact that we would not bump into Eva. The waiter who attended us seemed rather surprised himself that we had chosen to eat there, obvious tourists that we were, and appeared reluctant to hand us a menu, as if the real business of the place was the card playing going on just inside the entrance, near the bar.

There were tables with red-and-white-checked gingham cloths, unprotected beneath cloudless skies, and it was at one of these that we sat. Stars shone in competitive brilliance with rows of multicolored lights strung the length and breadth of the square. To be accurate, it was more a rectangle than a square, with benches and stretches in the center where old men played *boules*. Surrounding their night-lighted game were thick-trunked plane trees, brought there and planted for the shade they provided during the sweltering days. In their gray-beige speckled limbs little boys sat, round-eyed, impassive, knobby-kneed French owls, silent, observing the old men at play. Only the most skillful motion, as the heavy metal balls skittled to their marks, brought sounds from the tiny bird mouths. "Bravo," sang one. "Encore."

An orange cat, fat, overfed, lazed on the sidewalk next to a gathering of sparrows. Above us, birds chattered noisily, clubwomen before the meeting had been called to order.

After a sane appetizer of *crudités*, Skye and I were deep into our *moules*, mussels steamed in butter and onions, whole buds of garlic softening in their juices, a dash of crème fraîche added at the last. I suppose this would be an appropriate moment to give some detail of that career for which my mother had such disdain. Having buried my aspiration to be a poet, entombed it, rather, in my still-ambulatory shell, I decided to become a journalist. One of the women I most admire is Sarah McClendon, whose husband walked out on her when she was thirty-four, with an infant daughter, forcing her into the marketplace, where she became a newspaperwoman before it was fashionable to be feisty. Since then she has stood toe to toe with Presidents Johnson, Nixon, Reagan, letting them get away with no evasion, understanding how men are. Mine was not a destiny drawn toward Washington, although I match Dan Rather's frankness of gaze. But in the early days of my marriage, my longings were traditional: I assumed my first loyalty would be as a wife (which it *was*). So I did what I could do in San Francisco without it interfering with my obligations to Elliott: I wrote about food.

While still dealing with words, I felt food-writing would give me protective coloration, since no one is likely to tell you your observations on chili peppers are immature. I had a gifted friend who became a lawyer for much the same reason—he said it was unlikely that anyone would say he'd written a lousy brief. So does the world send its artists into caves, never considering how cruelly it can hurt the feelings of those most likely to have them.

Elliott was supportive about my choice, even encouraging, since it gave us evenings in some of the best restaurants while, I was later to understand, giving him access to some of the best waiters. It is a struggle not to seem bitter or small as you recap in your mind all the pert little waitresses you were too secure to worry about your husband finding more attractive than you.

My style has improved over the years, as I worked to give my topics more resonance than your usual food writer—one of my articles, "Feeding the Elderly," attracted a great deal of attention. And it had been noted by a particularly well-read friend

39

that with time and concentration I might achieve the verbal symmetry of a Mario Puzo, who writes about food as some men write about sex. In my mind, there is no contest between the two, nor any question in which coliseum I would prefer being champion. But in the absence of a better offer, I surrendered to the *moules*.

When two women have not seen each other for considerable time, and trust each other, the first thing they talk about is their disappointments, what has brought them to the not-so-pretty pass they are in today, before moving on to a brighter tomorrow. Like Persian rug dealers, Skye and I unrolled our betrayals, pausing to note the elaborate patterns in each, the flaws we should have understood were a part of the design, since only Allah is perfect. The food narcotized our grief, and the wine, a crisp, Provence rosé, cooled to a nutlike impertinence, loosened our tongues.

I had never known Skye to drink very much. After beauty her most notable characteristic was restraint. The clothes she wore were understated, as her voice was soft, modulated to a decibel so low you strained for her words, which effort on your part loaned them greater impact. I had seldom heard her laugh loudly—her pleasure sounded blown in glass, like the tiny crystal bells at dinner parties where hostesses seem hardly to want to disturb the help by calling for the next course. And if her laughter was subtle, more so was her sorrow. It sat like an unfavorite relative, benched behind her eyes, waiting for an opportunity to visit, even uninvited.

Socially acceptable feelings being furtive in her, or, at least, dealt with so discreetly, it was stunning to me, then, when she started telling me about Gerd, and what had, as they say, gone down between them. She spared no detail, and, fascinated though I was, I was also thunderstruck that this perfect person had these feelings, experiences, canals, and more amazing, could talk about them. I could only assume she was very drunk, and very human, the last being something we seldom allow honored friends to be, especially when we have put them on pedestals, a fitting place for a statue. My amazement must have been quite like that of the moviegoing public when Ingrid Bergman conceived out of wedlock.

She was laughing about a particularly lustful encounter they had had in Venice, where, apparently, love rises in inverse ratio to the city's sinking. Suddenly, startlingly, her great silver eyes filled with tears. "Why did he leave me?" she asked.

The words seemed to be without self-pity. It was a question, simply.

"Why?" she asked again. "His paintings were selling for fantastic prices. And he was always so scornful about money. Why would he marry Charlotte?"

"Well, that isn't money," I said. "That's a kingdom."

I suppose that was the worst thing I could have said. Or perhaps right then anything I said would have been the worst thing I could have said. She let go, and the tears flowed freely, as from the eyes of ordinary people, any attempt to hold them in ladylike check abandoned. Naturally that had to be the moment when the local paparazzo reached our table, the professional cameraman sprung from the spill of Bardot, cadging his living by intrusion. Snapping, the explosions of his flash like blows across Skye's tear-drenched face, he lurched and bent and hovered. She covered her eyes.

"Go away," I said. "We're not anybody."

He seemed not to hear, or understand, or pull back even slightly from the frantic waving of my hand as I tried to shoo him away from there like the pest he was. "Smi-le," he said, giving it two syllables, exposing his irregular teeth, John Carra-

41

dine trying to pose as an amiable person. "Bee-yu-tee-full smile."

I could suddenly see myself scowling from the front of Paris Match. These people didn't care who you weren't. Like our own *National Enquirer,* all they really wanted was a terrible story. The most obscure person in the world could get a headline if his tale was shoddy enough. So, just in case some unattached Italian nobleman was meant to fall in love with my picture, I smiled, and to my shame, started posing.

He gave me a card, marked "St.-Tropez Photo," with an address. "Too-morr-roww," he said. Then he was off to the next table, photographing the couples there, the first stop on what would be a complete tour of the square.

Nearby, a waitress giggled, a throaty laugh, filled with cognac. From among the clatter of the chattering birds one raised his voice in song, a winged Pavarotti, undaunted by his assignment to the chorus. In a far corner of the square the strains of a classical guitar sounded, some beggar, perhaps, trading the remnants of his training for a glass of wine. And through it all, like a bass note, came the sound of Schuyler's crying. Disloyally, I felt a spurt of absolute joy. A symphony of summer. Reverberations of life. The photographer with his hustle had reminded me that this was a holiday, replete with potential souvenirs. I had enough to remember of faith breeched, and hopes corrupted. Look where I was, look where I was.

Two long-limbed young men in black tie stumbled past our table, laughing, uttering obscenities in French. *"Merde,"* said the taller of the two, his foot caught in a tangle of awakened cat, shrieking its outrage. Behind the two boys—on second look they were closer to boys than men, with that gangling look boys have when they are still forming, craning their necks the better to see what was going on up there in the adult world that made it so desirable—came a very drunk young woman. Her long yellow hair was disarranged in the frizzed current fashion, rock singer with finger in the light socket, is how I tend to think of it. Her shoulders were totally bare, with that slightly emaciated and slumped quality the very young seem to think attractive. She wore a blue dress cut from sweat-shirt fabric, gathered above her spare breasts, hanging straight to the floor, where glistened, like Dorothy irretrievably far from Oz, red Lucite shoes. There was a slash up the side of the dress all the way to her hip, and as she passed our table she flashed a glimpse of thigh, so pale, so white as to seem almost luminous. Although I am not an expert on the inner thigh of women the pallor of it seemed to echo that thigh earlier revealed on the hill below Skye's ledge, and I wondered if hers were not the same legs so listlessly spread at Mittri's party, and if so, which of the young men with her had grounded her.

She seemed to lean toward the taller of the two, as I imagined any woman would have. His face had about it the slightly rounded, rosy glow of cherubs on chapel ceilings, which beauty was intensified by the long, light line of his lashes, cloaking the blue of his eyes. His hair was corn yellow, curling slightly under just above the collar of his tuxedo shirt, open at the throat, revealing a wide neck with a prominent Adam's apple. His hands were large, big-fingered, a gauge my mother always had for how impressive a man's other extremities might be. I had frequently seen her holding hands with men for whom she had little regard to begin with, she who had no particular penchant for affection. What it turned out she was doing was measuring.

The trio seated themselves noisily at the table next to ours, whistling for the waitress, calling out for wine. The tall one flashed a rakish, winning smile, as though he would win service like the loyalty of subjects, Prince Andrew back from the Falklands, beaming innocence and a potential for scandal that everyone would know wasn't his fault. There was such obvious civility in his bearing, it made all the more incongruous the rude stories he was telling. In spite of my limited French, I could tell they were rude, because of how raucously his friends laughed, and the deepening color in Skye's cheeks.

"They're talking about Charlotte and Gerd," Skye said softly to me. "They've been to their party."

"What are they saying?"

"I don't like to eavesdrop."

"I do," I said, annoyed that I had not paid more attention to Professor Sidi. "It isn't fair that you understand and won't tell me."

Cocking her head so her shiny dark hair swung softly, all of a piece, to her right shoulder, she half-closed her eyes, in concentration. "Apparently," she murmured, "he's having an affair with Charlotte. The one who's talking."

"The beautiful one with the Adam's apple," I noted, Howard Cosell to her Dandy Don. While he was still trying to fool me, maybe even fool himself, Elliott never missed a televised football game. Loyal as I was, in my own way as hypocritical, I pretended to enjoy the sport, acting as though it did not shred my sensibilities, that Cosell's voice did not rape my ears. Perhaps if I had run screaming toward that tube, and done to the image of football what it has done to the souls of American women, Elliott and I might still have been together, watching "Masterpiece Theatre." The football strike of '82 seemed to me not so much an index to the greed of the players as a sign from the gods that wives had suffered enough.

"He's saying terrible things about Gerd," said Skye, the long graceful rise of her neck growing flushed, heat moving up visibly from her breast.

44

"What?"

"Let's go." She signaled for the check.

"He's an asshole," the tall one was saying now. For a moment I thought a miracle had occurred, and my mind, like a computer, had magically tuned into the language, offering instant translation, although the magnitude of my understanding the French for "asshole" stunned me. Professor Sidi had taught us a little *argot*, French street talk, but in my recollection it had gone no closer to the gutter than *flic*. It took me a beat to adjust to the fact that the fellow was speaking English, and a very fine English, too, except for his choice of word. That is to say, he did not pronounce it "asshole," but "ahss-hole," making it into the King's English, deepening his association in my mind with the young Prince Andrew, which would, I suppose, have made it into the Prince's English. If the Prince would ever consort with ahssholes, much less call them by name. But then, if a cat can look at a King, a Prince can look at a porno star, in which case he would certainly know some assholes.

"Bien sûr," the little drunken frazzle-haired girl was saying, straining up to kiss the young man's neck, its Adam's apple so prominent as to seem phallic. Normally I would have tried to be more reserved when observing, putting a menu in front of my face, or pretending to blow my nose while watching a couple dance through love's preliminaries. But as this was to be my spectator summer in all things sexual, and I had already seen the same young woman *in medias hump*, I saw no point in being discreet, so I stared. Having noted the phallic simile in my mind, I was fascinated to see if, as she teased her tongue along his jugular, his Adam's apple got hard.

"You don't understand," he said, and took her chin between

45

his fingers, pushing her gently away. "We English are not like you froggies. When we love, we love."

"*Bien sûr,*" she said, her lips in a puckered moue, fashioned by the pressure of his hand.

"I can think only of Charlotte, dream only of Charlotte." His fingers moved to the back of her hair, fraternally, tangled in its curl. "She is everything to me."

"*Bien sûr.*" She started to undo the rest of the buttons of his shirt, and twirling her pointed tongue through the light hair on his chest, trailed her face slowly south.

"He uses her. But *I* love her."

"*Bien sûr,*" she said, in that same monotone, just before he pressed her face down into his lap.

"Let's get out of here," Skye said, springing to her feet.

"Don't you want dessert?" I cried lamely, and was instantly ashamed. But she was already out of there, and, being the perfect guest, I had no choice but to follow, without a backward glance. Well, maybe one.

To FALL asleep in a strange bed, in a strange land, with the heart and the mind wounded by a loss, is not an easy assignment. Although I appreciated the privilege of where it was I was stationed to experience my pain, the pain was no less real for the fantasy of the locale. To pick a cactus pear bursting with ripe, red juices growing unexpectedly along the side of a road you never thought you would walk on doesn't mean the needles won't stab you. Despond kept bubbling up in me, unexpected, random, unconnected to any conscious thought. As angry as I was, as disappointed, I had loved him, we had loved each other, he had seemed to appreciate me, laughing at the things I said and did that seemed funny, soothing my hurts, never planning

46

on being my biggest one. Little belches of sorrow kept coming from me as I lay there, like a motor that had seemed to die, but every once in a while turned over.

I got out of bed and went to the window, looking at the stars, trying to think about things eternal so that the ephemeral nature of love would seem less wounding. I had never seen so many stars. Above glowed the diadem of the Seven Sisters, the marquise-shaped cluster from which those who ruled our collegiate destinies took their name. When we were undergraduates, there was no scent of disclaimer or antagonist in being at a woman's college, no sentiment of second-class. Rather, like our male equivalents in the Ivy League, there was a sense of pride at being accepted where it was mandatory to be sharper, nonsensical to feel any inadequacy or apology because of sex. What surprises we were in for later.

A gray-bellied bird circled the air in a clearing between the trees, batlike, indefatigable. Birds did not circle at night at home, not to my recollection. Were they different in France? Did the air that allowed so many stars to show also affect the boldness of the birds, color their night behavior? Was everything changed because of where I was, the exotic rock where I did my hard time, Alcatraz for disappointed lovers? While in my neighborhood at night I might have heard a woman calling "Harvey," here in the dark green stillness, a man's voice cried out "Jean-Pierre . . ."

I went back to bed. Something pricked at me. I slapped my arm, turned on the light, and started at the sight of my own blood on the bedsheet. In the middle of the blotchy red circle lay a squashed insect, with huge transparent wings. Somehow, in the death of a mosquito that has your blood in it, there is more pleasure in revenge than itch. So, I decided, should it be with an ex-husband.

47

THE BEACHES of Saint-Tropez offer a number of surprises, the most commercially notable of which is the absence of Bain de Soleil, leading one to the conclusion that it must be the sun that gives that Saint-Tropez tan. The intensity of the heat cooked me as it browned, adding my own basting scent to those around me, coconut oil, cocoa butter, toasting flesh.

I must say the spectacle of all that skin was a little hard for me, although I have a number of good friends in Mill Valley, and have spent some of the most nervously memorable evenings of my life in hot tubs, where I thought the worst thing I had to fear with Elliott was Group Sex. The beach at Le Club 55 was wide: nearly a city block of finely pebbled, coarse sand stretched between the restaurant and juice bar, and the water. To see every foot of it covered with near-naked bodies, oiled and browning, like barbecued chickens displayed in a deli, was, to say the least, disconcerting—albeit fascinating in the case of French breasts, which looked quite different from our own, coming to definite points. Perhaps that is a manifestation of the French attitude toward sex, so much more direct and matter-of-fact than ours. Even in the midst of a sexual revolution Americans are forever noting that they're in a sexual revolution, still not taking for granted that sex is a normal part of life, which it certainly appeared to be on that beach.

Just above the line where the water broke in gentle, lapping waves, little more than a wash of foam, a man walked naked, his penis trailing dejectedly in noncircumcised fashion, as though proud as he might have been to so display it, it was just the tiniest bit depressed; brass yellow curls of hair grew down his back, and on his buttock cheeks. A little girl shrieked with that curious combination of terror and pleasure that little girls seem to feel, as her mother carried her into the sea. By the edge of the water an African walked in native mufti, blankets for sale thrown over his shoulders, hawking purses and ivory bracelets, a round silver tray held like a shield in front of his breast. In the near distance a honey-skinned blonde maneuvered between the sunbathers, a large pink scarf with Lurex threads wound round her slender body into a sarong. From her left arm waved another scarf, like a rosy sail, caught in the wind of her grace, advertising what she was selling out of the basket she held with her other hand. Serenely, interrupting her peaceful progress only when someone inquired of her, she made her way up the beach, waving, and vending. How wonderful, I thought, to be that silent and beautiful, your whole being a presentation of what it was you offered, and only getting stopped by those who were genuinely interested.

The sand was too coarse to walk on, scoring the bottoms of my feet like pumice stone, uncomfortable to lie on with just a towel. The club rented out mats, umbrellas, and, for true shelter from the blistering rays, *paillotes*, small open, hutlike affairs with thatched roofs of rolled, dried straw set atop four wooden poles, so you had the illusion of Tahiti. It was from underneath one of these that we stretched, Skye with a big, floppy hat covering her face.

I sat up on one elbow, the top of my suit still on, as though the whole population of that beach was waiting for the generous spectacle of my breasts. All around us were breasts, near us a couple with his nearly as big as hers, next to them a woman with beautiful uniformly brown breasts, her flesh the same rich dark as the nipples. A blonde woman with newly lifted breasts, scars underneath their centers a deepening pink, displayed the mutilation as proudly as the perkiness.

Since we had turned our backs on each other so often getting into uniform for lacrosse, I felt self-conscious about looking at Skye. There is a peculiar modesty among Americans, no matter how close their friendships are. The frankest among them can reveal agonizingly personal secrets and still be embarrassed about undressing in front of a friend, as if nudity always equated with desire, except in California. In other words, it is okay to bare your breast, as long as you don't bare your breast.

Still, even without turning my head, I could not help but see. Skye's breasts were surprisingly apple-round and opulent, considering how well and flat-chestedly she wore clothes. Little splinters of sunlight fell on the sand near her head, eating through the thatching. She sprawled on her *matelas*, her body a portrait in odalisquean composure, breasts curving softly toward her upper arms, nipples rosily brown, a shade darker than the flesh around them.

"I'm thinking of having them made bigger," she said, from underneath her hat, as though she could sense me appraising her.

"What for?"

"Maybe he likes bigger breasts. Maybe that's why he left me." She didn't smile when she said it.

RIGHT AFTER he married Charlotte, in a wedding that the New York *Times* had characterized as a gathering of the Fortune 500 (two of them members of Schuyler's own family, too thick-skinned not to attend), Skye had enrolled in business college. Like any good woman obsessed, she imagined the flaw lay in herself. What Gerd had always criticized in her was her sense of "unreality," by which she gathered he'd meant inherited income. Perhaps, she thought, it was her lack of hardheadedness, her failure to be more pragmatic that alienated him. Blind to the logic of Charlotte's fortune also being handed down, albeit in huge disproportion to the rest of the heiresses in the world, encompassing as hers did shipping lines, railroads, liquor franchises, and furs, Skye took new heart, and, second-winded, sailed off into becoming a self-made business woman. Clever enough to master even those techniques that clashed with her humanism, shortly after receiving her MBA she went to work for IBM. At that moment, our paths recrossed. She seemed pale and filled with doubt, as though her sensitivity were in the process of being reprogrammed, computerized. Shortly after that I was happy to hear that she had quit that job and opened a boutique.

With her eye for style and decor, and her new head for business, it was not long before there were airy little stores with white walls, and multicolored glass ceilings, like different-flavored Jello squares, in several cities, two of them in Europe. I was partisanly proud of her. It is always reassuring to know that there is blood and brains in at least one of those women Harper's Bazaar is always foisting on us as examples, because of how well they wear clothes.

As I walked through the streets of Saint-Tropez later that afternoon, I was keenly aware of the male eyes on me. It is easy to tell the French eyes, because they are particularly gleeful and friendly when looking at a woman, unembarrassed about appraising even when they should be otherwise engaged, that is, with a woman already on their arm, or, the back of their motorcycle.

Quite pointedly, I gave my attention to the faces of the buildings so I would not seem to be searching the faces of men. Vines grew up and over *pension* doorways, wound around rustbricked Roman arches crowning the cobblestoned streets. Laundry hung from second-story windows, in neat arrangements on triangular metal casings and pulleys, held by brightly painted clothespins so it looked like decoration, multicolored flags above the streets, proclaiming a holiday of clean. Green leaves hugged entryways, like eavesdroppers straining for conversation. Little colored lights, opaque by day, outlined outsized restaurant menus, and arcades.

The scent of freshly baked *baguettes* and *ficelles*, crusty and hot for dinner, came from the open doorways of bakeries. In a room siding an alley, a baker's assistant with carpenter's tools measured out a huge rectangle of flattened dough, cut it into precise strips while his assistant followed, setting into each strip two flat pastilles of chocolate. A third followed them, pressed the dough closed and arranged it on a metal tray to be sent into the oven for *pain chocolat.*

Children played games alongside sports-shop windows, where white Adidas with ziploc laces proclaimed the universality of sneakers, and how much smarter they were in France. Small Renaults straddled the sidewalks outside clothing stores, which announced sacrifice sales, the one benefit of a depressed economy.

Through it all I wandered with something like confidence, shoulders back, chin high, eyes straight ahead, with the singleness of purpose we had learned to display during long-ago summers in Europe when our hearts were young and gay, instead of our husbands. Skye had suggested I go into town by myself. Since I was to be visiting for a month, the sooner I developed a sense of independence, the better. I told her I wanted to shop, which was only a little away from the truth. What I really wanted was to see the proofs from the previous evening. Like most women whose egos have been raked over, I was extremely concerned with how I looked, especially to

52

other people. The photographer's eye, I thought, would be cold and hard enough to give me a literal picture of myself. I walked up a side street, to which a gendarme had directed me, past a cathedral with its bells calling the faithful to mass, or, as it was France, the unfaithful, and went down the steps into STTRO-PHOTO, the cable address as indicated on the card.

Considering all I had been through, I was surprised by the freshness of the face they set out before me on black-and-white contact sheets, smiling up at me through the magnifying glass. Part of my problem is that the eyes are the windows of the soul —in my case, green, and a little too wide. My nose would also seem to be a window of the soul, or at least a vent, thin and upturned at the end, which gives you a certain sauciness, no matter how pert you aren't inside, or how impudent you don't mean to be. People see that kind of face and presume you to be flippant, simply because your features are, especially when combined with curly hair, and dimples. Still, at my age. I have considered having them filled in, like pockmarks, but silicone moves, and collagen is costly.

So caught was I in wondering how to spread a veneer of sophistication over that face (did Yves St. Laurent have a makeup base called Jaundice?) that I nearly didn't notice the man in the photograph at a table behind me, eating in the restaurant adjacent. I moved the magnifying glass toward me, increasing his size, and recognized him as the young man on the dock that first afternoon, with the maybe towel in his jeans. Studying him carefully, I realized how very tired I must have been not to pay him more conscious mind, a man as attractive as that, and wished that I could see more of him.

It occurred to me that the photographer, in his busy coverage of the square, might have paid the young man longer shrift.

So I turned the pages, and, indeed, there he was, a whole gallery of him, dark-haired, sunken-cheeked, his dark eyes extremely deep-set, nearly Indian they looked above the slant of his cheekbones. He glowered at the camera, as if he resented its finding him alone. I checked that carefully. There was no one else at his table.

"Well, what do you think?" asked a deep, pleasant voice behind me. I turned and saw the young man himself, as though I had stepped into the church on the way there, and made imprecation to whatever Saint it was who gave himself for Tropez.

"Three stars," I said.

"Really?" He grinned. The darkness behind his eyes disappeared, light and recognition taking its place. "I remember you. You're the girl at *Senequier.*"

"There were a few," I said.

"Not like you. Not honest."

I raised my eyebrow at that, or tried to. Whenever a man openly notes how honest a woman is, it is usually because he is trying to get her to drop her guard, by making her think he is honest.

"That was a pose," I said. "Who I really am is a black-eyed blonde."

"I like your disguise," he said.

I started up the steps. "Why are you rushing off?" His hand was on my arm.

"You're a little too perfect." I tried to move past him. He was very clean and, I thought, smelled of baby powder.

"Give me a chance. You'll find something about me that's less than perfect."

"I'm afraid I already know something," I said, and hurried out of there.

HE CAUGHT up with me outside the shop, and took me to *Senequier*. On the way there we passed what appeared to be a not very nice hotel. Standing in the doorway was the tall, young Englishman, looking like a painting by Brueghel of a country celebration, joyful, rambunctious, down to the massive erection in his pants. And in his arms was Charlotte, her pale, lined face alight with love, and/or, as I was later to learn, just a little champagne.

THREE

SHADES OF EARTH, TOUCHED by different intensities of sunlight, were the buildings of Saint-Tropez. From clay pink to deep terra-cotta, they rose two and three and four stories high, like sentinels guarding the harbor, stiff, unblinking. An occasional renegade pastel invaded their ranks, a lavender house, its first floor sheltering a boutique or beauty parlor. Against the stationary stucco faces played the pageant of yachts and small sailing vessels bobbing gently at anchor, covered with bright marine blue canvases, as though to challenge the brilliance of sapphire sky.

The yacht basin was cut like three sides of a trapezoid into the belly of the village, the far quay lined with houses, in front of which were tied the largest yachts, those owned by the mothers of movie producers, or cadged temporarily by press agents. Directly across, slantingly parallel to that quay, artists set up their easels, painting the scene opposite, or displaying already finished paintings, most of them of the houses on the quay and the boats. One had the feeling, observing, of seeing both the depiction of reality and the reality itself, too good to be a reality.

A gray-white seawall bordered the harbor, protecting it from winds and currents, with an opening just wide enough for vessels to come and go. Near the massive parking lot, for those who made a more conventional entrance to the port, were rows of portable stalls, where lively young girls in trendy costumes, blue lipstick, black fingernails sprinkled with sparkles, hawked costume jewelry, keychains, rip-offs of Rubik's Cube, fat ball-point pens with women painted on them. Turned upside down, the women lost their clothes.

The main quay, connecting the far one with the artists painting it, was lined with bars and restaurants, banks for the quick exchange of currencies, kiosks draped with mass-produced versions of the costlier clothes sold in the chicer boutiques closer to the square, souvenir T-shirts, soft drinks, thickly rich ice cream. In front of that circus of indulgences passed the informal grand parade, those who found it more blessed to be looked upon than looking.

On the sidewalk in front of the great line of yachts, serious-faced dropouts from the School of Beaux Arts held twenty-minute portrait sittings, sketching tourists' faces with skillful sweeps of charcoal, giving the least of their subjects gleams in their eyes, proof that art could endow qualities life did not. A lone bassoonist played a Mozart concerto, piping his affection for the instrument along with the music, inspiring the air with the conviction that there was no ill wind, if properly blown. At his feet, his bassoon case lay open, ready to receive offerings.

My dark-eyed stranger had seated me in the back row of

Senequier to protect me from the sun, which by that hour was slanting directly above the basin and below the level of the cafe awning. Nothing was between us and the glare but the masts of the yachts. There was a stillness on the harbor, in spite of the people and music—stagnant heat, a light mist forming just above the horizon. Helping me seat myself as comfortably as I could in the red-painted canvas chairs, he sat beside me, our elbows touching. He signaled for the waiter, and without asking my preference ordered a bottle of Château Minuty, Cru Classé, rosé. His action might have seemed less than considerate if it weren't for my familiarity with the wine, and its quality, which is crisp, original, light-bodied, and subtly aggressive, as, apparently, was he.

"I thought you were French," he said to me, the highest compliment he could pay, since the assumption carried not only my place of origin, but hints of sophistication and sex, nipples showing through see-through blouses. I did not quite believe him, since my face is a map of America, missing only a flag popping out of my forehead like a cuckoo clock proclaiming me red, white, and blue.

Still, I stroked him back. "I thought you were Italian," I said.

He smiled. I could sense the irony behind it, anyone's thinking he was Italian. "I am Italian," he said.

"You speak excellent English."

"Italian from the Bronx."

"You still speak excellent English," I said, and we both laughed.

The wine came. The waiter did an elaborate little dance, opening, offering the cork for smelling, pouring just enough to taste and express approval. It was an impressive display, really, considering we were in shorts and the day was still bright upon us. More fitting would have been candlelight, black tie, which

59

was perhaps the very incongruity that loaned it such a serious air, especially on the waiter's part, as accustomed as he probably was to serving cassis and negronis and wine by the glass.

"*Santé,*" said the dark-eyed Bronx Italian, and raised his glass and his eyes to me.

"*À la vôtre,*" I said, having been there now three days, one of them unconscious. I considered it a milestone in my awareness that I at least knew I was unconscious for one of them.

"What made you cry?" he asked me. "When I saw you here the other day?"

"I don't even know your name," I said. "And you ask me for something as intimate as the truth."

"Don't tell me if you don't want to."

"You have a name?"

"Sal," he said. "Sal Boglio. The *g* is silent."

"Then how come you pronounced it?"

"I want you to fix it in your mind. B.O.G.L.I.O." He chalked it on an invisible blackboard. "What's yours?"

"Tess," I said.

"That's all?"

"Well, I have a last name I'm just getting rid of, and I haven't decided whether to go back to the original or not." He was looking at me with such genuine interest, it was all I could do not to spill the whole squalid tale right there on the table, except that I wondered how it would make me appear to him, unwomanly, a patsy. Besides, it was still August, not yet the off-season, when people tell the truth.

"What was the original?"

"Laughton," I said. "The *g* and the *h* are silent."

"Go back to it," he voted. "That's a good name."

We sat in silence for a few moments, sipping our wine, taking a measure of each other. There was something exceedingly spare about him, muscular as he was, an economy of movement in his gestures. I tried to think who he reminded me of, and decided it was Humphrey Bogart. I was about to tell him so when I recognized that if I said he reminded me of Humphrey Bogart he would think I was old enough to remember Humphrey Bogart.

"Is he why you were crying?"

"Who?" I asked.

"This person whose name you're dumping."

"Yes."

"Do you still love him?"

I was unprepared for such direct questions. I looked away.

"I'll bet he still loves you."

The warmth with which he said that, the sympathy, carrying as the words did the implication that Sal would be powerless to do otherwise, deeply touched me. Fortunately I had determined to practice emotional restraint for the summer, as well as sexual abandon, deciding to model myself on Skye. The composure, that is, that she had demonstrated over the years I had known and admired her, and not the unraveling she had been through the night before at dinner. I managed to keep the tears within my eyes, ladylike, hovering just inside the bottom lids. It gave the end of the day an extra sheen beside the one on the water.

"You've been hurt," he said.

"My God, you're perceptive," I said, and laughed because I was finished with crying. It was a holiday.

I REMEMBER when I was just starting into my teens, the book we all read was Mrs. Aadland's revelations about her little girl, Beverly, and Errol Flynn. As we lived near the Main Line, adolescent girls did not masturbate, or, if they did, there was even more humiliation and shame in the act than if God himself had walked into the room and called them Onan. Two thirteen-year-olds of my acquaintance had been caught at summer camp, legs spread, diddling each other, all the more shocking in that they weren't even particularly friendly. The most the rest of us did, and only when we were best friends, was scratch each other's backs. At any rate, the two of them were shipped off to school in Switzerland, at opposite ends of Lake Geneva. I thought about them more than my affection or regard for either of them warranted, usually when I felt yearnings I was too embarrassed to satisfy.

Masturbatory fantasies being un–*de rigueur* in our thigh of the woods, we did the next best thing we could do, and that was dream of movie stars. All of us had hopes of being whisked away sexually at fifteen, preferably to a yacht, by a celluloid god, albeit not one so old as Errol Flynn. We devoured the book, found it all the more riveting for being intellectually endorsed: a critic at Esquire had compared it to Evelyn Waugh. That meant we could read it aloud to each other on the telephone, a more civilized way of touching each other between the legs without risking being caught by a counselor.

Florence Aadland's tone struck me, poet as I still was then, halfway between fan magazine and biblical. What impressed me most, even as I tried to pretend I found it funny, was that she knew from the moment her girl was a baby how sensual she was going to be, because, as she said, she had about her "the scent of musk." As filled with doubts as teenage girls are about themselves, as loaded with fears and confusion, to my own share of uncertainty was added unexpressed envy that I did not have the same potential. So far, I had found no advantages in life from either education or tenderness, and wished that the

62

universe had handed me instead an appetite for ignorance, and perfume coming out of my parts.

Since I did not carry myself that scent of musk, I spent a lot of time trying to sniff it out in males. As my mother measured her success by the accomplishments of her partners, so I tried to increase my own feeling of self-worth by attaching myself to boys, and gradually men, who seemed to have an aroma of horniness. I would hope to find it in my nostrils at parties, going so far as to put musk mothballs in my closet so that when summer was over my clothes would hint of passion rather than naphthalene.

The scent itself, available in perfume and oils, was too heavy for me. But I gifted Elliott with it when we got engaged, and in the second year of our marriage actually bought Kamasutra Oil of Love, musk flavoring. As even a tyro in sexual experimentation knows, this, when applied, heats up with a touch of the tongue. At the time, I was extremely self-conscious about ambling into X-rated boutiques. My first visit to one was marked by the spectacle of a very old man holding a vibrator, rattling from head to toe, crying feebly: "How do I turn this thing off?" Understandably, I regarded sexual exploration as a setup for mortification. But the way our society has gone, some of the nicest women on the Peninsula get together for what they themselves have labeled Fuckerware parties, where a representative comes equipped with Benoit balls, edible underwear, all manner of lubricious devices for sale, along with free counseling. So my depravity, it turns out, just about dovetails with Alice's, whose only flaw was curiosity once in Wonderland.

But the wish to come across the fragrance of musk in its purest form on someone's flesh has stayed with me. Like a childhood trauma, unremembered, which, when cracked into conscious recollection makes the patient walk, I have known since early adolescence who would have the oars to my boat. Sitting there at *Senequier,* the press of tourists forcing Sal and me into closer contact, I began to sense a subtle fragrance overwhelming the baby powder. Something within me started moving, deep, almost imperceptibly at first, like the mysterious stillness in the ocean before Ahab cried, "He SOUNDS!"

I strained to concentrate on the sunset, thinking from that to draw strength to resist this man, at least until dark. But the sun had moved beneath the glaze of mist, stretched across the horizon like a silver ribbon and I could take no direct energy from it. "What are you wearing?" I asked him, trying to sound casual.

"Wearing?"

"Underneath the baby powder. What cologne?"

"No cologne." He looked at me squarely. "Just me."

I suppose he saw how I was looking at him. Even I could see how I was looking at him, from inside my eyes. "Why don't we go someplace else?" he asked very softly, touching my hand.

I shook my head. The sun seared the silver ribbon pink. His touch burned my fingers.

"Why not?"

"I couldn't handle any more disappointments."

"What makes you think you'd be disappointed?"

I shrugged.

"You don't look like a cynic."

"I don't look French, either. You just said that to make me feel sexy."

"Well?"

I tried to find something fascinating in the bottom of my wineglass. "It worked."

"Then why don't we go someplace else?"

"No." I tried to sound firm, but there were reverberations

64

in my belly. Below, to be accurate. I was afraid he would hear it in my voice.

"What did you mean before? About your knowing something about me that was less than perfect?"

"It was only idle speculation," I said, not wanting to put him on the defensive about his organ. As many articles and books as we may read, and may be published, about the size of a man's penis being irrelevant to sexual satisfaction, I think the man has yet to be born who can handle having a small one. Penis envy, it seems to me, pertains more to men than women, since I noticed on those evenings in the hot tubs that it was the men who nervously eyed each other's equipment, as though in some kind of contest. Probably Freud had a little one, the reason he invested it with so much importance, and dreamed so often of his mother. Maybe he had a penis only a mother could love.

Those appendages appear to be, rather than an index to a man's strength, the key to his vulnerability. Impressive as they may be at full staff, it usually takes someone else's running it up the flagpole to make them salute. Perhaps one reason women were for so long made to feel inferior was that men needed a feeling of power to get it up, lording it over them, as it were. But in even homosexual graffiti, the little I have seen, reproduced from a bathroom wall at Andy Warhol's, there were only gigantic erections, some being stroked, some acrobatically shoved, some swallowed; but at no point, no matter how delicate the proprietor, is there ever a fragile cock. Not that these things are important to me, but I figured they might be to Sal, so best not to say anything.

"Idle speculation on whose part?" he was saying tenaciously. I understood about him already, as brief as our acquaintance was, that he didn't let things go very easily.

"No one. Forget it. It's not important."

"I'd like to know," he said, teeth clenching, visibly toughening, like a little boy in a schoolyard who wanted the name of the tattletale. I guess the manliest of them is some part little boy, even when he has about him the scent of musk.

Just at that moment Charlotte Windeler Halsey Mittri and her young Englishman sat at the table in front of ours, or, more accurately in Charlotte's case, collapsed into a chair. Still perceptible beneath the creased fabric of her face were the fine bones that had made her the most admired debutante of her day, sad remnants of a beauty saluted by poets and newspaper columnists alike. Her blonde hair was pulled back from the sides of her face, so tight it appeared to me to stretch her eyes, making them a little too wide-set, fishlike, as if she wanted to check, in some eerie physical manifestation of paranoia, who was watching her from either side. Her hair was drawn into a sparse chignon at the back of her neck. I imagined that when her hair was full as her coffers, the style might have been becoming; now it looked straggly and thin. There seemed to be a certain stubbornness to her continuing to wear it in that fashion. Wealth can't buy you beauty or youth, but it can certainly buy you hairdressers.

"What will you have, my darling?" asked the young Britisher as the waiter approached them.

"Maybe . . ." she hesitated, as though she were really thinking about it, her great black eyes, once so celebrated, and portraited, flat now, like a shark's ". . . just a little champagne."

Sal signaled for the check. "Let's go," he said.

I leaned toward him and, in hushed tones, explained who Charlotte was, my relationship with Skye and her betrayal by Gerd. Sal did not seem to grasp why any of this precluded our leaving.

"Spying on people is not my idea of a good time," he said.

"Be patient. Please." I leaned back in my chair, the better to watch Charlotte.

Her hand as she lifted the champagne to her mouth looked translucent, the veins in it blue, risen slightly, like rivers in a relief map. She drank the contents of her glass very quickly, and, almost as quickly, it was refilled by the young man, who looked at her with the soft-eyed ardor of a Saint Bernard finally come upon someone to rescue. I suppose the only thing more powerful than the scent of musk is the scent of money. Or mother.

THERE IS a melancholy to dusk in Saint-Tropez, like love affairs ending. Beyond the chatter, a solemn quiet wrapped the harbor, the tone that sits on the spirit when bright colors fade. Comforting in a way, but nonetheless a kind of death.

The Englishman, or Yorkshire lad as I had begun to think of him, redolent as he was of a certain sweetness of spirit, pretty and so young, had moved his chair very close to Charlotte's, the better to stroke her arm, and, apparently, solace her *malaise*. She seemed quite jittery, her eyes darting about in a manner that might have indicated fear of discovery had she not flung the two of them headlong into the best place in the fishbowl.

He rubbed the back of her neck. She smiled at him, the line of her lips less drawn than the rest of her face, indicating that there, at least, she had welcomed some practitioner of rejuvenation, with a needle or twelve, to keep her kisses in full flower. She rested her head against the boy's shoulder, as though they were both teenage sweethearts, instead of just one of them.

Adultery to me is still nothing I can take for granted. I am always stunned when people who have made a sacred promise break it with such apparent ease. Even in the movies, when the wife is away too often, I like to believe, along with her husband, that where she is, is bowling. So to see a partner in a famous marriage and on such a high level that they have not even been in People magazine under "Couples," trashing her vows in public, made me uncomfortable and angry. Especially as that pairing had been so devastating to my friend.

"Let's go to dinner," the Yorkshire lad said.

" 'Stoo early," said Charlotte.

"Then let's get married." He traced the line of her throat beneath the collar of rubies and diamonds with his very long, very flat index finger.

"Don't." Her eyes were half-closed, the look on her face exceedingly languorous. It took me a moment to realize his other hand was out of sight beneath the table.

"Divorce Mittri," he whispered.

"Let it alone," she said, in a tone so edgy I was not sure if she meant the subject, or what he had hold of.

"He doesn't deserve you."

"I've asked you not to talk about him," she said. "He's a great man."

The young man laughed. "How can you keep saying that when we both know . . ."

She took her glass of champagne, and, I think, tried to throw its contents at him. But she was not very well coordinated, or she was drunk, or maybe, as I had intuited the night before, she was crazy. Whatever the explanation, it was the glass and not just its contents that struck his face, shattering, opening a gash below his eye.

There was blood all over his face, and a look of terrible surprise. Charlotte screamed, and stood up too quickly, knocking her chair over, covering her eyes, as if some unknown assailant had done this to them, Lee Harvey Oswald loose on the Riviera. She reached blindly behind her—for what? A Secret Service man? A waiter rushed over with a towel. In seconds it was soaked through with blood. The soft murmur of conversation amplified to an excited buzz. All around people were standing and straining for a look, violence apparently giving their lives an immediacy that beauty could not. Amazingly, Sal was on his feet, taking a towel from another waiter who stood gawking.

"Press this against your cheek, as hard as you can," he said to Yorkshire, demonstrating an authority I was unused to, that most of us are unused to, I think, once we grow up and realize that the adults who gave the orders are now us. "Get him to the emergency hospital," he told Charlotte. She took Yorkshire's hand, the one not pressed against the towel, and the two of them stumbled out of there.

I sat quietly for a moment, trying to compose myself and deal with the sudden electricity I was feeling, more powerful even than that evoked by the scent of musk. It was not what had happened at the next table that had caused it, the sight of blood bringing blood up in me, but rather Sal's reaction, the takeover quality he had, scoring him so obviously a Man in Charge. I suppose all of us would like to have a cavalier who fights for us, but more subtle is the search for one who can save us when we are wounded. Since so much of life seems to be accidents and mayhem, it is reassuring to know there are still some rescuers, not all of them with the fire department. To see the dispatch with which Sal had leapt in to handle the situation touched my G-spot, this newly phenomenal thing they think they have just discovered in women. Women themselves have known all along that they are capable of feeling a tug in their soul and their vagina at the same time.

"What do you do?" I asked Sal.

"I'm an undercover man," he said, and grinned at me.

"Ha ha." I tried to sip my wine, but the glass was empty.

"I'll prove it to you," he said, and took me somewhere where he could.

THE MIRACLE of the *nouvelle cuisine*—besides the delicacy with which it is prepared, the acuteness of color and taste, the integrity of even the puréed vegetables set into little mounds or clever designs like leaves on a riverbank—is the way it is served on the plate. Nothing touches. Rather it is landscaped, an exquisite garden through which the tongue is free to wander, and the palate can cleanse itself in between tastes just from the freshness of the design.

So it was making love with Sal.

There have been a few men in my life, some experiences chokingly dry, overcooked, some as delicate as truffles only to be marred by the overpowering, soggy pastry wrapped around them. Elliott, for the best part of our life together, was a *paillard* of beef, properly seared—rare inside, but with a beefy burnish. Along with his main dish were offered up unexpected savories. But he was, in the main, old school.

Sal, however . . . Sal was *nouvelle cuisine* to the core—light, delicate, attractively turned out, with first-class ingredients.

He took me back to his hotel, off the same little road as Skye's villa. It crossed my mind for a second to run him past her for her approval. But I dismissed the notion, partly because I wanted to feel adventurous and mature enough to make the decision myself, partly because I knew without asking her that it was too soon and wanted to avoid the censure in her eyes for tumbling so quickly into bed with this mysterious stranger. It is only by acting quickly enough that strangers stay mysterious.

I already knew more about him than I should have known to make it a truly European encounter, the kind Brando had for his Last Tango, a colossal marathon fuck every which way simply because a woman was looking at the same apartment. I knew Sal's name, where he was from, that in his childhood, probably, someone in the schoolyard had hurt him, making him disproportionately angry when he didn't know the source of the rumors, or what they were. Insight can be a terrible thing to have in an affair, and I tend to be cursed with insight. Especially when it can do me the least good. So I thought it best to get to our bestial level as quickly as possible, lest I saw him too clearly.

I was due for an adventure: life seemed to owe me a positive charge. So rather than fill myself with doubt, and second thoughts, I did not even signal him to turn into Skye's driveway. I felt a little guilty that I was about to enjoy a tender, muscular embrace and she had no one. That is, she had only the *one,* that beacon signaling to her, across the years, and now from next door. With herself too discreet to shine her radiance in return.

In some corner of my mind, I suppose, I was afraid that she might not like Sal, that this direct, understated man with his gently muscular torso, so well defined beneath his T-shirt, would not meet with her approval. But it was my decision, after all, my judgment that had to be called upon. What Skye would think was beside the point. One woman's meat is another woman's *poisson.*

So we turned up the gravelly driveway to his hotel—Les Bergerettes it was called, filled with intimations of all things diminutive and three starred. The outside of the lodgings was white, freshly painted it looked, even by night-lighting, with red-tiled roof and Moorish arches, as though it had been whisked there from Spain. Flowers blossomed everywhere, impatiens clustering fuchsia and candy-striped pink and white by the doorway. Down the steps to the left I could hear children laughing and splashing in the pool. The tiles of the patio felt cool even through my shoes. He guided me by my elbow, his fingertips gentle on the soft flesh of my inner arm.

The desk clerk hardly looked up as he passed Sal his room key. We went up the stairs. There was a stillness in the hallway, a solemnity that seemed almost churchlike. A monastery might flourish there in the off-season. But not in summer. Not in summer, and not this evening.

We moved inside his room. He did not turn on the light. The drapes were opened onto a small balcony, and from it we checked out our particular portion of the local heavens. The stars shone even brighter than the evening before, in seeming greater profusion. And that constellation that had gleamed so brightly above me, the Seven Sisters, now appeared as a cluster that became the bottom part of a diamond heart that glittered in the sky, a giant valentine. It shot me full of wonder that God might be a sentimentalist.

Sal moved around me, touched my throat with his lips, without yet touching me with his hands, sipping me like a gentle, stingless bee, moving his mouth up over my chin, kissing the dimple in it, working it with his tongue as though he would draw honey from it. Then his mouth was on my mouth, eating across the outside of it, tasting without biting, supping on me. And his tongue was on the inside of my lips, exploring, tasting, making a tour of my teeth before plunging into the warmth behind them, dancing with my tongue.

He touched the outside of my breasts with the flats of his

72

palms, pressing me closer to myself, his fingers only finally touching my nipples, through my clothes, as with an afterthought, drawing them out to full attention. He reached between my legs, gently, again with the flat of his palm, as though he wished to reassure, affirm, stroke me into soft flames rather than intrude.

He started to undress me, easing my clothes away from my skin, pulling my shirt up over my head, slowly. My hands were more reluctant than his, passive, not reaching to undo the button at his waist as he did mine, partly because I carry with me the fear that aggression in women might be interpreted as masculine, and partly, and more to the point, out of nervousness that what Eva had said that first afternoon might be the truth. If it was the truth, I was in no hurry to verify it. No hurry to do anything, because of what was being done to me with such an infinity of care.

He touched my breasts, directly now, moved his palms and fingertips along the outsides, circled softly, bent to caress them with his face, his cheeks, running the silkiness of his hair across their burgeoning tips. "They're beautiful," he said, and leaned to kiss them, suckle them, press them between his hands.

He moved me to the bed and drew my shorts down over my hips, taking my pants with them, slipping off my shoes. He lifted my feet, one by one, gliding his tongue over the instep, making a darting circuit of my toes, pressing the moist pointed tip of his tongue in between them, so that it was all I could do not to cry out.

And cry out I did, finally, little moans, choking up in me like the grief I had felt less than twenty-four hours before, like the mourning for love, transmuted magically now to longing. I had never felt anything quite so tender as the ministrations he gave my toes, filling me with hunger to be ministered to in other

73

places. And as though he could hear me, feel inside my brain with the same sensitive probing he had my toes, his tongue moved up the inside of my leg, made warm circles behind my knee, trailed up my inner thigh to my center.

He spread me with his hands, and made the same journey through my nether lips as he'd made in my mouth, caressing first with fingertips and tongue the outer folds. Then with extraordinary slowness, teasing with the tip, his tongue made a circuit of the inner folds, coming close to, but never touching, my own pink tip, which I could almost hear cry out loud for wanting to be taken. Finally it was in his mouth, gently pressed between tongue and teeth. He worked it for what could have been no more than seconds, when I was shot into eternity, throbbing around him, and he was plunging inside me with his tongue while his thumbs massaged my mons.

I could feel him smiling against me, hear the short muffled spurts of satisfied laughter that he had so pleased me mingling with expressions of my own pleasure. Then he was hurriedly taking off his own clothes, and moving himself over my body, his mouth maneuvering up to my lips, while his hand stayed below.

He kissed me, plunged my own flavor into my mouth with his tongue. From somewhere far away I could hear music. Or maybe it was from inside me. His fingers played me like a harp, pulling my strings.

"You're so warm." He reached for my hand and moved it downwards. "So juicy. Feel."

I resisted. It seemed, even for one of my (I thought) experience, a curious wrinkle, touching myself when there was someone else who was doing it so brilliantly. Shades of the banned tales of little girls in summer camp and sin suffused me, along with the sad apprehension that Eva had been right about him, that he lacked the means to fill me up, and needed help. Reluctantly, I let him guide my hand and urge my own finger inside me. And it was true, how warm and wet I was, so moist and lush I could almost feel my own pinkness.

But it wasn't true about him. Eva was totally wrong. He was in me suddenly, gigantic. Gigantic, and silkily strong, like satin and velvet with iron within strapping my insides and my finger. I was coming again, so fast and hard I couldn't even hear myself moaning this time, couldn't hear myself screaming with bliss, bliss and relief. Such relief. Because you never knew. You just never knew what was waiting for you.

He was grinning down at me. Grinning, and pumping and laughing, coming to his own shuddering rest, crying out as loudly as I had, unashamed, filled, emptied. He eased himself down against me, rested his head against the side of my throat, kissing it with pleased, relaxed, affectionate kisses.

I could feel tears coming out of my eyes. Joyful tears this time. "She was wrong," I said, triumphant. "She was *wrong.*"

"What are you talking about?"

"Nothing," I whispered, and rolling him gently off me, kissed the slightly sweaty mat of the hair on his beautiful chest, ran my fingers through it. "Isn't it wonderful?"

"I don't understand what you're talking about," he said, and stroked my hair.

"That's good," I said, and kissed his lips. "We're only in trouble if we think we're speaking the same language."

WHEN WE had rested, the kisses became less affectionate than seeking. I sat him up on the edge of the bed, not afraid now to treat him as I felt like treating him, to do as I wanted, to honor him with the same loving attendance he had paid me.

75

I put my lips to the tip of his member, drew it into my mouth, caressed it with my tongue, felt it lengthening and hardening.

"Do you mind if I turn on the light?" he asked me.

"Not at all." I drew my head away while he switched on the lamp. His face was alight with expectation, what I would have interpreted, had I been foolish enough to be sentimental, as the beginnings of genuine affection for me. But I was prepared to take it for just what it was, and that was pleasure that we both were taking from and giving each other. So it was enough that his face was lit with what it was lit with, and his cock was aglow with the same anticipation, bobbing in the air a few inches from my face, purpling at the tip, summoning me to pay court.

I circled the head of it with my tongue, pulled back to see its deepening color, as though my touch had the power to darken it, as it made it grow. I looked up to see his face, and he was smiling at me, proprietarily, as though pleased with my progress. He touched the outsides of my cheeks with his hands, clenched his fingers in my hair, as I plunged the growing length of him deeper into my mouth, gliding him past my tongue, and into my throat.

With my fingers I touched the base of him, explored with the skin beneath my fingernails the hair around his shaft. It was silky and delicate, not the harsh and wiry hair I had expected. How much of this man was not what I expected. I moved my fingers around and beneath, and gently threaded his satiny balls between my fingers, stretched for the line of skin between scrotum and anus that a friend of mine says is the true ecstasy spot for men, and massaged it softly, while above me, as if to confirm the truth of that claim, Sal moaned.

I moved my head back and forth, stroking him with my mouth, taking the enormous length of him as far as I could into me, while I rubbed the base with my fingers, feeling true joy

76

from the gratification I knew I was giving him, from the sighs, from the sweet clutch of his hands on my hair, from the stirrings in my throat. Then he was reaching under my arms, and lifting me up onto his lap, spreading my legs, bending them on either side of his so I was straddling him. He thrust himself inside me, and lifting me, pumped me up and down until we spilled into each other.

He lay back on the bed, with me still astride him, my legs still bent, my head on his chest, my spirit exalted, but sore. Because when it was over in the past, never so rich, never so full, I had always whispered "I love you," as had Elliott. A habit, I guess, like reaching for the Kleenex. But habits, as we know, die hard. I was not used to making love with a man without it ending with words of love. No man I had ever made love with had ever given me better cause to feel grateful.

So, compromising, a burst of giving in my throat, I said, "Thank you."

And Sal whispered, "My pleasure."

WHEN I got home, Skye was a blonde. "I did it this afternoon," she said. "Maybe he likes blondes. Maybe that's why he left me."

FOUR

CHANGING THE COLOR OF her hair had been a lot easier than piercing her ears. Our senior year in college Gerd had mentioned casually to Skye that he thought women were sexier with pierced ears. She could not even wait for vacation to effect that improvement but had gone straight into the village near campus, managing to find the only gypsy in New England, and had had her lobes run through. I remember her with those awful pieces of string in her ears, like a child from an underdeveloped country, which is what, I'm afraid, some of us really are.

She had suffered enormous pain in the process, as the gypsy was, in addition to primitive, arthritic, and her hand was neither steady nor firm. One of the myths of so-called civilization is that ear piercing doesn't hurt. I had mine done at the smartest jewelry store in Union Square by a registered nurse with a gun. The agony was so exquisite, in the worst sense, that I screamed, and would have refused to let her do the other ear had I not turned and seen the next customer waiting in line, a four-year-old girl, looking at me with eyes filled with pity at my immaturity.

Skye had not even had the mercy of modern brutalization. A week later, her gratuitous holes had begun to fester, and by the time she went home that spring, were virulently infected. Only quick action by the top skin specialist in Boston had managed to save her lobes, which were badly scarred, the reason she always wore her hair over her ears. Her doctor had suggested she correct them with plastic surgery, but Gerd relished the imperfection. Like a truly enlightened man who will kiss the stretch marks left by his wife's baby, understanding that he was the cause, Gerd tendered to the minimutilations, paid them affectionate tribute whenever they made love, and sometimes even when they didn't. I would see them walking sometimes on campus: he would have his hand around her neck in what looked at the time like a standard collegiate show of boy-girl affection. It was not until the night she had too much wine and unloosed such a plethora of erotic detail that Skye made clear to me what he was doing at those moments. As aphrodisiacal an instance of public sex as I've heard.

She did not hold him responsible for the unnecessary pain, much less the scars. There is such a thing as a victim's mentality irresistible to an oppressor, and God knows he had cooperation. It is my understanding from a former Hitler Junge that I met in Saint-Tropez that summer that it had never occurred to him as a boy that Jews were not animals. Apparently, in that long-ago Germany, one spoke to them like dogs: "Get up, Jew," they would say, even the German children, and the Jew would get up. That same unquestioning obedience was why they went so unprotestingly into the ovens, and the real explanation, it seems to me, why Israel is so intractable in its refusal to put up with any abuse. Israeli children, watching films of European Jews being herded to oblivion, ask "Why didn't they fight?" So fighting is what they never stop doing now. A nation alchemized from victims to warriors.

No such alchemy had taken place in Schuyler. The tacit agreement to lie down and, if need be, die at the whim of the subjugator was apparently deep in her bones, Protestant though they were. From her earliest consciousness of the difference between the sexes she had been willing to place her destiny in the laps of men as Greeks would have the gods, her hopes clambering up over their knees like a toddler aching for comfort. The world seemed to her to be caught in some mythic imbalance, which only a masculine arm guiding hers could put right.

While some women struggled to affirm that their only requirement for survival was themselves, Skye remained convinced that the measure of womankind was man. Her own excellence, her beauty, her kindness, her wit (with respect to everything else but Gerd) were qualities from which she took little sustenance. I would like to say she was a throwback to her mother's generation, and my mother's, and propose that she was going against the flow. But in view of what has happened to the women's movement, and how many girls still want to be Miss America, I am afraid that she was, in truth, a mirror for her day.

So there she stood, her newly golden hair tumbling around her remarkable face, Pandora having opened the box in which the gods' gifts to mankind were contained, letting them all escape, save hope, and Clairol. I would have felt annoyed with her were it not for the fact that she looked even more lovely as a blonde. Besides, I was flushed with beneficence because of my adventure, a visceral understanding of exactly how much good a good man can do you.

I did not mention Sal to her that evening. She was so caught up in her own panic about whether or not she had done the right thing to her hair that she did not even ask me where I'd been. Not that she was vain, self-centered, or frivolous, like women who obsess over such matters. But she could only concentrate in the library if she was in her accustomed cubicle, and became nervous during finals if she couldn't sit in the seat she was used to. So imagine having someone else's head.

She was, however, enough of a kneejerk perfect hostess to ask me if I'd had dinner. I told her I wasn't hungry, which was true. I know the theory is that obese people are sublimating a sexual urge, which would seem to be verified by the fact that I couldn't eat another thing.

I related to her the terrible scene at *Senequier* between Charlotte and the young Englishman and watched her grow quite pale beneath her tan. I could almost see her brain martialing itself, which it is somehow easier to do with blondes, as she worried her lower lip and wondered aloud if she hadn't waited long enough to make her move.

THE NEXT day, a parade of manufacturers' representatives and assistants, fabric designers, panderers to popular tastes whose functions were undefined, descended on the villa, bringing sketches and samples of what would be the following spring and summer collections carried in Skye's boutiques. Being unfamiliar with the machinations of such businesses, I assumed that all these clothes were for her the natural extension of the change that had begun with her roots. If blondes had more fun,

I would also assume they had bigger wardrobes.

Nymphs and elves and others whose category I will not define, for fear of sounding racist, fluttered about her as though she were Titania being readied for Oberon. Which reminds me that the reason I canceled my subscription to Ms. magazine, in spite of its occasionally crisp prose and my great admiration for Gloria Steinem, especially her hair, was an article in that publication discussing *A Midsummer Night's Dream,* arguing that the real problem between Titania and the King of the Fairies was that she had her period. I could envision a whole generation of Shakespeare scholars searching their Kittredge editions for menses, attributing Lady Macbeth's hand-washing to the absence of sanitary napkins in ancient Scotland, and her confusion at encountering her first transsexual ("Who would have thought the old man to have had so much blood in him?"). One could trace Juliet's innocence to the fact that it hadn't happened to her yet ("O, swear not by the moon!") and the entire tragic action of *Othello* to his revulsion at womanly functions ("O bloody period!"). Sometimes, they do get carried away.

Not that I am unsympathetic to the struggle of the feminists, though I do wish they would conduct it in a less fire-breathing manner, since anger never got anyone anywhere. As men are so fearful of their feminine side, it would follow that American women, whose favorite heroine is still slyly manipulative Scarlett O'Hara, are fearful of their masculine side. The defeat of the ERA, although in the main due to the rigid conservatism of our country, is also, it seems to me, partly the fault of those who came on too strong, not allowing the willows of the South and Midwest to feel any sense of identification. Women who have for generations been bred to flutter have to be spoon-fed personal courage, not have it rammed down their throats, particularly by those whom they could not in a million years consider "sisters."

So, in my opinion, the women's movement pretty well fucked itself, which, come to think of it, would probably please a number of its members. Still, there are side-stream tragedies to the defeat of the ERA, not the least of which is that it freed Phyllis Schlafly, by her own account, to concentrate on what she considered more important work—i.e., taking sex education out of the schools and fighting the advocates of a nuclear freeze, since, she actually *stated*, with everybody listening, that the atom bomb was God's gift to the United States. Where was the Pope when she said that? Where were the bolts of lightning, or Paul Newman at least, asking her who, then, gave it to Russia?

It embarrasses me for God sometimes the people He has declaring themselves on His side, and humiliates me for women who they sometimes find among their ranks. The only consolation is that there are men who are even dopier, and those not even the Seven Dwarfs, but members of our own Cabinet, such as the Secretary of Energy, who said that in the event of a nuclear war he wanted "to come out of it number one, not number two." As if anybody could come out of it anything. The Hertz of the Holocaust. Who are these people in whose slippery fingers is our destiny?

I apologize for allowing such weighty matters to intrude on what is essentially a summer's tale of Romance on the Riviera. But perhaps these concerns will further clarify why I soaked up that vacation like gravy with Wonder Bread. And why we all might be well advised to do the same, while we can.

At any rate, there sat Skye on the middle of one of three catty-cornered white couches in the conversation pit of her living room, with reams of silk, bolts of linen and cotton unfurled around her, like offerings to a pagan princess whose religion was clothes. The intense concentration she gave each piece of fabric shown her, the furrowed brow with which she regarded every sketch proffered, every hand-painted Japanese screen design to be transferred to sweat shirt, might have led some *parvenu* to conclude she took it all very seriously. But I had been present when she made her valedictory address at graduation—summa cum laude she was, which seemed excessive at our college, where to graduate at all was honor enough. This is based on no overblown opinion on my part, but the philosophy of the administrators, who elected not to have a Phi Beta Kappa society on campus, since, they said (even the most modest among them), that to be at our school was the equivalent of being Phi Beta Kappa anywhere else. Is it any wonder we felt no sense of apology for being women, and that many of the men visiting our campus had sheepish expressions on their faces as though they weren't sure they were good enough to pay court, which attitude prevailed until they became engaged to us, and we simped into surrender and gratitude.

The keynote of Skye's speech was a quote from F. Scott Fitzgerald, before the booze oozed in, that the test of a first-rate intelligence was the ability to keep two opposing principles in mind at the same time and still retain the ability to function. It seemed to me that Skye had done that most of her adult life, accepting the idea that she could be anything she wanted but that none of it counted for shit unless she was something *he* wanted. That is as clear an illustration of the Fitzgerald thesis as any I've encountered, and would probably have pleased its originator, who might have had doubts about himself but always knew Zelda was brighter, except that she let him run her life.

In the midst of all that soon-to-be sartorial splendor there was a ringing, followed by energetic knocking. Two of the elves, along with Skye's valet, hurried to the door. A gust of very brisk air came into the room with Eva, who disposed in one sentence of her approval of Skye's new hair color, and her annoyance with me for not having called on her to plan my schedule. I assured her I had been having a wonderful time. She seemed displeased that I had managed it without her.

"Saturday night," she proclaimed, the general martialing the troops. "The amusement park near Port Grimaud. Special fireworks. You come."

"Port Grimaud?" I asked.

"The little village you pass on the way here. Like Venice. Little houses on the water, with each one has a boat."

"I didn't see it," I said.

She looked into my eyes to check them for blindness. "How did you come here? By the moon?"

I might have taken exception to the intolerance of her manner were it not for what was happening with Skye. She had lost all interest in the activities in her living room, fashion, flusterers, and had gone someplace else inside her head. Her pale gray eyes were suddenly opaque, as though a shutter had been closed behind them to keep the world from looking in, reserving her privacy of thought.

"Excuse me," she said mindlessly but with automatic good manners, like someone brainwashed whose hypnotic trigger had just been cocked but whose breeding could not be eradicated. Patty Hearst remembering to curtsy. In a moment she was back in the doorway. Having apparently set the next step in her plan, she signaled to one of the sketch artists to join her.

"What do you think?" she asked me, holding out a creamy piece of vellum after everyone had gone. On it was inked in exquisite calligraphy an invitation to attend the fireworks that Saturday evening at Luna Park.

"Who sent it?"

"No one. I'm sending it to them. Gerd and Charlotte." She tilted her head, which seemed much more vulnerable now, and a little emptier for being blonde, and checked the script and the wording. "It looks very impressive, don't you think? I can't imagine their not wanting to come, it looks so official."

She took my silence for censure. "I can't wait forever, don't you see? And it isn't as if we had mutual friends here who would ask him over, or even as if I could meet him somewhere for tea. He never goes out in the daytime. His painting, you know."

"I thought maybe he had to stay in his coffin till nightfall," I said. I will confess to a certain lack of tolerance in my attitude, a sense of personal violation at his abandoning her. There had to be something dark in his spirit to make him leave Skye, and for a hag. Vampirism seemed an easy answer for those of us who do not wish to dwell on the complexity of human longing.

"He isn't like that," Skye said, smiling, a mother dismissing a child's arson as mischief.

I was not convinced. Any man worth his salt, indeed, all that were not worth their salt, should have fallen in damp little crystalline heaps at her toes. The American Dream, that is, not the one that imagines everyone can be a success, but the dream of the country itself, the quixotic cornerstone of the nation's foundation—belief that the good guys could win—should certainly have extended to the good women. No one had more to offer than Skye. So why had it not worked out the American way? Why had he not been caught up in the fancy, even if he was a refugee?

The facts of his history were more or less known to me, as they were to most people who read, whether through straightforward pieces in the New York *Times Magazine,* persnickety profiles in the New Yorker or cover stories in any number of publications that at one time or another became obsessed with him. Mittri had been born in Almería, Spain, in the early thirties. Actual records of his birth had been destroyed in later attempts to hide him from the Nazis. His parents had fled Franco, settled in Italy, which accounted for the Italianization of their name (originally Merita), and had passed a few contented years in Selvole in the Chianti district of Tuscany, his father tending vineyards while the son was taken on frequent excursions to the Uffizi Museum in Firenze, where he fell irretrievably in love with art. When the war began, his mother smuggled Gerd into Switzerland, entrusting him to the care of a foster family, returning to help her husband in the resistance. Both parents had disappeared shortly afterwards and had never been heard of again. He had finished his schooling in Switzerland, and with the coming of peace to the planet, such as it was for as long as it lasted, had journeyed to Harvard with a scholarship and a new identity card.

Doubtless there was much in that young history to inspire suspicion and fear. But consistent acceptance had followed, with universities on both sides of the Atlantic courting him, first with offers of education, then employment, enough material comforts to subsidize his body so his spirit could flower, enough free time so his painting could flourish. I can only assume that women were as ready to extend their favors as universities were. So what in his saga would explain his inability to let Skye love him? Of course, there is no accounting for taste, and even less accounting for behavior.

Skye moved to the window, fixing her bright gaze on the irresistible spectacle of the Mittri villa, the hot sun gilding the new champagne shine of her hair. "I've waited so long for the perfect occasion," she said. "I was afraid when you told me last night what had happened that I'd waited too long. I mean, if Charlotte's starting to get violent, and in public, God knows what she might try to do to him when he leaves her."

There seemed no doubt in her mind that that would be the natural unfoldment of things, nor any fear that Charlotte's next target, and with something deadlier than a champagne glass, might be Skye. It amazed me that she could seem so assured about the direction everything was going to take, when she didn't even have the courage of her own coloration.

"But this is perfect, don't you think?" The honeyed glow from the soft wave that fell near her cheek seemed reflected on her skin, like a statue exposed to so much sun and rain that, marble though it was, it had come to resemble flesh. "A carnival! With fireworks! Spectacular!" She backed away a little from the window, as if her joy might be too effusive, radiate all the way to the Da Vinci Bunker and flush him out, spoiling the surprise.

"Fun," she said, softer now, a wistful note creeping into her shadowy voice. "Innocent. The way we used to be when we were first together. Luna Park. What better place for us to find each other again?"

"I don't want you to get hurt," I said, mature, as always, about other people's actions and destinies.

"Oh, pooh. You sound like my shrink."

"Are you still seeing him?"

"No," she said. "He committed suicide." She looked at me fondly. "You worry too much, Tess. Just be happy for me. Be happy because I'm going to be happy." And lifting her lovely tanned legs, she did pirouettes around the room, adorable in her enthusiasm, her certainty that what she was doing was dancing, and for joy. I caught a sudden fuzzy flash of that same Zelda Fitzgerald who had been such an inspiration to Scott, and so little to herself, posing for pictures in her tutu, waiting only for the right stage to begin her concert, going mad because the music for her solo never started.

SATURDAY NIGHT in France is not like Saturday night in the U.S. of A. As sex is a part of life for our *cousines* across the sea, so Saturday night is a part of the week, with none of our cultural adolescent hang-ups about not having a date making you an old maid. As one of my electives, the Alma Mater having waxed truly liberal, I was permitted to take a course in American songwriting, which is, I think, an index to the American character, as runic writing in caves is to its civilization, or lack of it. Squarely at the feet of "Saturday Night Is the Loneliest Night of the Week" I lay our national hysteria about dating, more powerful even than the suicides wracked up by Billie Holiday's recording of "Gloomy Sunday," a far better song. This panic seems to have made its way into the blood of the generation that heard it, to be passed down in the genes, since their daughters are no more relaxed even never having heard the tune.

In France events of importance are set on Saturday night simply because the next day everybody can sleep late, while intending to go to church. And women come to Saturday-night occasions with women friends, just as they dance with each other, because they enjoy the movement and the music.

We drove to Luna Park near Port Grimaud in Skye's car

with Sal at the wheel, since with Skye's mentality it would never occur to her to drive when a man was present. Ms. magazine, while I still subscribed, had articles on how many things we were trained to think men can do better, when we, with practice, could be just as skilled. At one point in my struggle to join my sisters, I sent away for fairy tales to read my niece that were sponsored by Marlo Thomas, in which the heroine was a carpenter. A friend of mine, a psychologist, holds a workshop in what she calls "rehearsed helplessness," to undo automatic turning to a man, whimpering, "Oh, I can't do that." But in my opinion there are some things men *do* do better than women, naturally, and one of them is drive.

When Brando was making *Last Tango in Paris*, Bertolucci, the director, instructed him to "think of yourself as an extension of my cock." As outrageous as such an instruction might sound to one not in the Actors Studio, or used to talking dirty, it seems to me that dictum might be applied to driving. In other words, men do think of cars as extensions of their manhood, as witness all the shifting of gears accompanied by grunting motors that we see in Burt Reynolds' movies. Anyway, she let Sal drive, and I, for one, enjoyed the ease and authority with which he did it.

I could see her checking Sal out in the rearview mirror, and knew she wasn't quite sure about him, even as well as he drove. They'd had no real exchanges, none of those moments of truth where you can evaluate someone's character and see that he is worthy of your best friend's interest. They'd met only twice, briefly, once when he'd come to take me to the beach, and once when he'd picked me up for dinner. Both times he'd politely invited her to join us, and she'd been polite enough not to accept. When we were alone she had asked me a few questions about his background, like where had he gone to school, and

91

what did he do. I had answered rather saltily that such things were unimportant, since I didn't know. She seemed now to be appraising him for some sign of nobility, placing a value on me that she could not, apparently, place on herself.

She sat in the backseat of the car, taking those last moments to compose herself, having planned every word, every gesture of the meeting, when she would smile, then take Gerd's hand. Recrimination was to be no part of her presentation. Undoubtedly he knew he'd been a bastard—there was no need to bring it to his attention. Negative feelings only made a person angry. So there was to be no pointing of fingers, only the reaching of hands.

She had hired a messenger from the village rather than send her own valet to take Gerd the invitation, rolled up like papyrus, beribboned, sealed with wax and a gorgeous imprint she had found at a local antiquarian. We had watched from behind the white drapes of her living room while the messenger motorcycled up the Mittri driveway and rang the doorbell.

Gerd came to the door himself. I heard Skye's sharp intake of breath. From our vantage point he no doubt looked much as he had during our undergraduate days. His posture was proud, as it had always been in the classroom when we studied Art under him, in Skye's case literally. The slump he had displayed in the presence of her parents on graduation weekend was, apparently, a stance reserved for times when he was not sure of himself. He looked very sure of himself now, standing at the doorway to his villa, his exceedingly broad shoulders square, the golden cap of curls that softened the dark, furrowed character of his face still golden, a slight silver cast underscoring.

I was unable to see his face, to check if his eyes—I remembered how penetrating their look was but could not recall their color—were still clear, demanding a cogent answer. Nor could I make out at all his most compelling feature, his lips, which I recollected vividly, even though I hadn't been interested in him myself because he belonged to Skye. He had a way of looking at you when you spoke to him, right at your lips, so you became extremely conscious of the movements of your mouth. When the time came for him to speak you would, as a reflex, look at his lips. They were generous and dark pink, set in a kind of pout, his bottom lip turning out and under slightly, showing a little of the inside, smooth and shiny, and a paler pink. I always felt slightly uncomfortable when I had a conference with him. As relaxed as I *thought* I was, bald sexuality made me nervous, and I was always afraid he might kiss me. Or might not. It amazes me that any girl lives to be a woman.

Now, there we were, in Skye's car, Sal at the wheel, on our way to the most significant meeting since Yalta. Skye was wearing a pale gray jersey shift the same exact color as her eyes, Gerd's favorite color on her. It clung softly to her body, eased over her widely spaced breasts, hugged the lightly musculatured line of her shoulders. She fingered her champagne blonde hair, convinced that in its tawny tones lay the key to the equation. *Cogito blonde, ergo sum* what he wants.

Just before we got to Luna Park, she told Sal to take the right-hand turn off the roundabout, and we exited toward Port Grimaud. Sal stopped in the parking lot.

"I'll be just a minute," Skye said, getting out of the car. Drawn by some need she did not explain, picking at a wound she preferred not to let heal, she ran across the main bridge that arced up and over into the town and disappeared through the cosmetically antiquated gate. In a few moments she returned, her cheeks flushed, eyes red around their rims. "It may be like Venice," she said softly, her voice lightly choked with tears. "But it's not Venice."

I wondered what it was she had seen that had moved her so, or failed to see. What specter of that other city, which seemed a metaphor for beauty vanishing, its buildings sinking in the sea, had risen to haunt her. And, more important, why had she gone out of her way to rouse the ghost?

LUNA PARK was turned out for the night with the conspicuous sparkle Skye was, and a great deal more flash. I had never been to a rural European carnival before. But I imagine we have been sullied for simple spectacle by the genius of Walt Disney, just as the slick comfort of Cadillacs has tended to spoil us for Peugeots. Rides elevated to Art form, amusements raised to Total Experience, as Disneyland and Disneyworld have made them, sours our taste, and clouds our eyes for Ferris wheels and the merry-go-rounds of less "developed" civilization. I have a friend who took her small children to Switzerland for Christmas, where they saw at the end of a funicular ride high in the snowy mountains what they took to be another artistic rendering of the Matterhorn. They came away thinking that Switzer was the greatest man since Disney.

This carnival had about it a diminutive sweetness for all its hustle, a simplicity of spirit in bottles to be knocked over, ducks to be shot. Electric bump-em cars sparked against the night. Children threw darts at balloons for prizes. There were octopus rides and caterpillars, vehicles for modest thrills.

Beneath the revelry I could sense a certain tension, little wrinkles of worry around the edges of the smiles of those who ran the concessions. I had read that attendance was off by a third at the great American amusement parks. Everything that happens to us on a Disney scale seems to come to those across the sea a little while later, scaled down; my own version of Reaganomics, or the Trickle-Over theory. So I wondered if the carnivals of Europe were not in for their own rough ride.

Sal held my hand. If those who labor so industriously over women's G-spots could bear to tear their attention away, they might find an equally responsive area in the human hand. Especially when it has not been held enough in childhood. He warmed my palm, the touch of his flesh firm along the lines of my fortune: heart, destiny, life. He bought me caramel ice cream. Ice cream had become another playground for us, duels of the taste buds to the death, between hazelnut, cassis, and caramel. Caramel had won. Now the task was to find the finest of all the caramels in Saint-Tropez, a search which had led us to Popovs at the port, through parlors, past outdoor stands to open windows, behind which ancient sisters mixed their own by hand.

He approached our mission with the seriousness of purpose and deadly humor Mort Sahl did the conspiracy theory, and I was crazy about him for that dedication. Crazy about him for a number of reasons, not the least of which was the way he helped me work off the calories. There are flowers that bloom in unexpected places, so fragrant and lush to the senses they make trivial the fact of whether ivy has climbed up a man's dormitory walls. Of course I still didn't know for sure it hadn't, since it would have been jejeune to ask where he went to school. But I knew instinctively he would have let it slip, or fall into a conversation, had he gone to Harvard or Yale, since Harvard or Yale men usually do.

With the two of us trailing close behind, Schuyler pressed through the crowds, searching for that well-beloved face, checking the set of every broad pair of shoulders, looking for someone tall besides the clown who went by on stilts. We were sure Gerd would not come there until after dinner, and no one in Saint-Tropez who adhered to local social customs dined before ten. It was only just past eleven, so there was little likelihood of his having arrived before us. But Skye was already wracked with fears that she had missed him, that he had come and gone, Sleeping Beauty awakening to find the Prince had ridden off, and without her.

"The fireworks are set for midnight," I reminded her. "I'm sure that's what they'll come for."

"What if they don't? What if they don't come at all?"

"Then you may never see him again," I said with an attempt at joviality, "unless you roll down the hill outside your window."

"That wouldn't be a good way for us to meet again," she said, gravely earnest, as though she had considered that option, and dismissed it.

She had refused Sal's offer of ice cream, had only toyed with the food on her plate at dinner. Her skin looked incandescent in the glare of the colored, revolving lights, shades of blue and red reflecting from its flawless surface.

"There!" she said, her own color returning to her. I thought for a moment she had spotted Mittri. But what she pointed to was a Ferris wheel.

In her projected fantasy of reunion, it seemed he was to come upon her seated alone in a compartment of the Ferris wheel with an empty seat beside her. It was the most genteelly spirited rendezvous she could imagine, the most idealized place for a long-lost lover to come across his once beloved. Perfection. The motor turning, turning. His sighting her, still aloft. Her returning slowly to earth in front of him, where, churning,

churning, she would beckon with her eyes, her entire being. It would be a poem.

The only problem was, she hadn't been sure there would be a Ferris wheel. Even Eva hadn't known for certain. Now that it glittered in front of Skye, its lights shining, cages bobbing above her head, calliope music adding to the sound of the joyous shrieks of children, she looked restored.

The rest of her plan was comparatively simple. I was to act as lookout, waiting by the parking lot for Gerd, snaring him and bringing him to the Ferris wheel. Charlotte I was to get rid of by some diplomatic measure she left up to me. When I had found Gerd, I was to signal Sal, who, like the next member of a relay team, was to tap the old man running the machinery, letting him know this was the moment for which he had been prepared.

The preparation was taking place even as we spoke, and had to do with a purseful of change and notes that Skye was stuffing one by one into the old man's hands. They were nicotine stained and thick-fingered, the face above them no sharper. His mustache drooped with incomprehension, as Skye detailed instructions in what I'm sure was flawless French, telling him please, at receiving his signal from Sal, to stop the machinery where it would bring her gently to earth.

She struggled to explain to him that all she was doing was for the benefit of an old love, to surprise him, apparently assuming any Frenchman would be as fanciful as she was, loving love better than anyone. By catching him in the web of her fantasy, she thought she would ensure success. But he looked at her dully, the whites of his eyes yellowed, as though the cigarette between his lips had jaundiced his view as well as his comprehension.

I was growing extremely frustrated for her, as even I could

follow approximately what she was saying, the passion in her speech making it practically into crash Berlitz. Finally, in obvious desperation, she told him she would let him in on a secret. The truth was, she was part of a crew making a film. The cameras were out there in the darkness, and she needed his cooperation to make sure she was in the right place, on cue.

Well, the lie worked, as the truth seldom will. He nodded and grinned out into the darkness at the unseen camera, waved at his imagined audience. Skye climbed into an open compartment of the stopped Ferris wheel, and drawing the metal bar across her lap, prepared for her circular ascendancy to the stars.

WE STATIONED ourselves by the entrance to the park grounds, kissing occasionally there in the darkness, Sal's fingers in my hair, his wrists on the sides of my neck. Just before midnight Charlotte's Mercedes limousine pulled into the parking lot. I knew it was Charlotte's because I had seen it parked in the driveway of her house near the skylighted glass entryway next to the glassed-in living room and the glass atrium. It had occurred to me that her house was perhaps an explanation for Charlotte's behavior: understanding that people who live in glass houses shouldn't throw stones, she had substituted champagne glasses. But the car made no sense in the South of France, where half the places worth going to would be inaccessible in such a vehicle. Still, she seemed content just to be sitting inside it. I could see her face through the open window, and she looked almost peaceful.

The driver got out and opened the door for her. There was a man beside her, on her right, but I couldn't see his face. Then the front door opened on the passenger side, and Gerd got out. The years had not been kind to him, they had been magnanimous. His facial lines, so sad and deep in his thirties, had merged into a look of austere power, wise authority. Thick eyebrows shadowed his eyes, which I could see in the moonlit darkness. Yellow eyes. Cat's eyes. Reflecting a light that wasn't even necessarily there. It struck me as odd that I could have forgotten their color, as unusual and riveting as it was. I could only think I had had a hard time looking up from his mouth.

"Are you coming?" he asked Charlotte, moving around to her side of the car. His tone was patient, indulgent, which to me showed a great deal of restraint. Because right then the man next to Charlotte leaned forward and turned on the light. And it was the Yorky, a bandage over his cheek, a patch over his eye.

"Wouldn't you rather stay here and have a drink?" he asked her.

"Well," Charlotte seemed to consider. "Maybe just a little champagne." She sat back in her seat and sighed while the boy drew a bottle of Dom Perignon from a bucket of ice in front of them.

Gerd turned his back on the car and came in our direction, a scowl on his face. "Professor Mittri," I said, out of respectful habit.

He seemed perplexed. It had, after all, been eleven years since he'd had that appelation. He narrowed his wide-set yellow eyes, and peered at me. "Do I know you?"

"Tess Laughton," I said. " 'Seventy-two."

"Why, of course." His face softened into a smile. He held out his hand. I shook it. "It's good to see you."

"I have a surprise for you."

"Really?" He looked amiably curious. "What is it?"

"If I tell you, it won't be a surprise." Ahead of us, Sal streaked across the carnival grounds, an Olympic torchbearer of intrigue. We followed his trail at a normal pace, Mittri asking me whether I was enjoying the South of France and had I kept up my interest in art.

"Yes, and yes," I said, not wanting to distract him from the treat that awaited him by being too interesting.

We were almost to the Ferris wheel. A couple was getting off. High above us, suspended at the apex of the wheel, Skye's tremulous face, so tiny it looked up there, pressed against the metal window. Sal tapped the old man on the shoulder, the signal to bring the opera to its main aria.

The old man started the wheel. But just at that moment the fireworks began, huge pinwheels of multicolored lights exploding against a starlit sky bled pale by the fullness of the moon. Cries of wonder and admiration rose from the crowd. The old man looked up, riveted.

Skye was two cars away from earth, still moving at accelerated speed. "Monsieur," she called out. *"Attention."*

Sal hit the old man on the shoulder. He pulled his fascinated glance from the rockets and turned back to the machinery, grinding the gears too fast. At the level of our eyes Skye dangled, the cage of her compartment spinning, herself whirling inside it as if she were being wound into a cocoon. "Oh, please, make it stop, make it *stop.*"

Gerd stiffened at the sound of her voice. The great eyebrows raised. The car of the Ferris wheel in which Skye revolved unwound slowly, coming to a shuddering halt a few feet away from us. She looked out and saw him, and tried to smile.

"Gerd," she managed feebly.

"Schuyler," he said in bewilderment.

But we never found out what his exact feelings might have been at seeing her again, and blonde. Because right then she stumbled out of the car, and threw up on his shoes.

100

THAT NIGHT, she tried to commit suicide. Fortunately there was nothing in the house stronger than antihistamines, so all she did was sleep for a day and a half, and not sneeze for the rest of August.

FIVE

Had he lived, her psychiatrist might have told Skye the variety of anxiety dreams that can afflict women. For myself, I know it was always abandonment, a train pulling out of a railroad station with my parents on board, having forgotten me, their faces pressed blankly against the window matter-of-factly watching the scenery, oblivious to my screams and wailing. For Elliott (I include his fears in the feminine litany without meaning to be unkind simply because I learned that summer from Skye that the brain is two-sided and the right side, the intuitive side, is feminine, and Elliott dreamed right-sided) the greatest fear was falling. He awakened many times in the night during our marriage, covered with sweat, having cried aloud, his big body jerking in panic, clutching at the bedcovers. When pressed, he told me he dreamed he was in his mother's arms, and she dropped him. The cow.

103

Fear of the dark is one that stays with a lot of women no matter how old they grow or how familiar the territory in which they are placed in the darkness. And, of course, there is the great formal ball at which one arrives naked. I did that one night, when Truman Capote finally invited me. "I knew all along I was right not to ask you," he said, his eyes at the level of my breasts. Death, the universal fear, pales in comparison, because at such distressing moments in dreaming one wishes for death. Some others: getting your period in the midst of a garden party where you are dressed in white. Being chased off a cliff by a witch, usually the one from *The Wizard of Oz*, for those who are old enough. Sharks, for the new generation, with anxieties dictated by Spielberg. Sleeping through the final exam.

But with all these, and the other greatest fears (send me yours) there is nothing on the scale of terrible things that could happen that weighs in heavier than Skye's. A humiliation made all the more agonizing by the intensity of the love she was trying to restore, the passion they'd had when things were right between them. Better than right, she'd told me, the night she had too much wine. Perfection.

By perfection she did not mean that bloodless love that idealizes, touching only spirits, eyes, and, on extreme occasions, fingertips. She had drawn for me vividly how it had been with them in Venice. Too vividly, I say with a limited sense of forgiveness, since even if she did not idealize herself and her relationship with Gerd, I idealized her. For her to have toppled herself from the pedestal on which we had all placed her, with the force she did, and the velocity, too much wine or no, was shattering for me. The wealth of erotic detail in her account of the Venetian adventure, their most idyllic interlude, was at the time more shocking to me than was the sight of her weeping, having had too much to drink. Of course a short while after that evening I was to myself enjoy an experience of the flesh that lifted the carnal to poetry, or at least it felt so to me, and certainly between my legs. But I am only a person, and Skye was Skye.

Though subsequent events were to mellow me, I confess to a prudish embarrassment at the time, as when one first discovers what it is one's parents are doing in there with the door closed. To this day I am astonished at the intimate detail related. I can only think that, besides being drunk, she was trying to make the memory more real for herself, so she would feel less foolish at having devoted the time and energy and thought she had to recapturing this man. To justify, I suppose, the size of the torch she was carrying, stoking her own furnace with remembered heat.

From the very beginning she had promised not to love him. It was a vow he'd extracted from her when he took her the first time in the twilight after art lab. His own commitment was to art and painting, that was his religion, his bride. He could be unfaithful only if they both knew it would go nowhere. Naturally, she had agreed, lying; it was already past infatuation for her. But anything he wanted she was willing to give, including a promise that was even then broken. She swore it would be for her as it was for him, simply something to be enjoyed.

What he would not surrender in wholeheartedness he gave to her in body, in fillips of creative lechery that were, literally, stunning. Her scarred earlobes were transformed, at his suggestion, into her clitoris. So as they crossed the campus, his arm draped casually around her shoulders, he would toy with them till she came, often while passing the library.

But it was in Venice that it became hardest not to confess she loved him. Venice was a city for those who had to cry aloud that they were in love. They had gone there eight months after graduation on a side trip from Rome, where Gerd was using his grant from the Ford Foundation to study at the American Academy.

It had been Schuyler's wish to stay at the Danieli or the Gritti Palace, one of the elegant hotels, where one felt like one was eating money along with the spaghetti, *pasta al soldi*. Holidays were usually her treat because she could better afford them. But since they'd come to Italy, the hospitality had been his. There was measurable pride in him, a palpable pleasure at being able to entertain her, even though he'd always sworn he felt no obligation nor guilt because the generosity had been hers. She didn't want to interfere with his delight at being the one who paid, and so she stayed without protest where he suggested, the Saturnia Internazionale, a hotel not so much off the beaten track as on it, but unnoticed.

The hotel was a few bridges away from the main piazza, the principal virtue of the place being the view it afforded of the rooftops of Venice. The room itself, however, was small, so they spent relatively little time there. Mostly they walked the streets along the canals, as Gerd, with proprietary pride in what had been for a while, at least, his country, guided her through museums and palaces and restaurants.

They rested in the Piazza San Marco, listening to the violinists play in front of the numberless cafes, eating great dishes of ice cream in the pigeon-shadowed plaza. Even though Gerd had said the trip was to be a sabbatical he'd found some confreres one afternoon at a nearby table and challenged them to a contest, offering a free drink to the one who could best draw a figure that had no proportion, like puppets made by inept craftsmen. He had finished his rendering in less than two minutes, easily winning the drink. On the way back to the hotel he told her the same wager had been made by the young Buonarroti. "Of course," Gerd said, "it's all right for your figures to be shapeless when who you will be is Michelangelo."

At the time he was going through some crisis with his painting which Skye did not detail to me, except to say that it was not a good time for painters in general. Everything but painting was holding the attention of the art world, supported by an interested audience, focused on by the critics. It was the era of conceptual art, where an idea was documented, some act in a remote region photographed and the photograph displayed in a gallery: two chalk lines a mile long each, four hundred lightning rods in a field. Then there was earth art, trenches dug in the earth, spirals of salt crystals, all to be reclaimed in short time by nature, nothing that had a shelf life, no art as Gerd understood it. He considered it made a kind of sense, in a bizarre way, where the avant-garde was going. But not with him along. An artist, to stay in fashion, he'd said, would have to move faster than a greased bat in a world where a greased bat might soon be considered art. For a man to whom art was a spiritual endeavor it was, to say the least, dispiriting.

Gerd had taken his impetus and inspiration from, indeed actually studied briefly with, Hans Hofmann, the German painter who'd resettled in New York. With the German ability to organize himself, Hofmann had found a concentration of other European artists, Max Ernst, Mondrian, Chagall. As America had a tendency to do, it gobbled up these people, neglecting them at first, then overtouting them till nobody wanted to hear about them anymore. Moving from complete obscurity to commanding huge prices, the reality of the cash clashing with their poetic natures, they'd busied themselves living on the edge, killing themselves in car crashes and with drink. Laden with their ideals, the ambitions of the Bauhaus,

107

Gerd had found himself in an uncongenial marketplace.

He had not seemed bitter when he taught us. He was an excellent teacher, as his mentor Hans Hofmann had also been —a better teacher, some said Hofmann was, than painter. Mittri lifted the work of even those untalented at painting (myself). The one criticism leveled at him was that he gave too much attention to the past, too much art history along with the instruction, because nobody cared anymore why the "Primavera" inspired one to awe. The European tradition of honoring one's antecedents was over. One should just paint.

In Venice, Skye said, he'd seemed preoccupied, holiday though it was. They walked in the misty afternoon back to their hotel. Huge whipped-cream-like clouds hung low on the city, thick as the parfaits they'd had in the piazza, in as luxurious piles, hovering close to the rooftops, nearly touching the marble cherubs that huddled in the cornices. His arm was around her neck, fingers playing with her earlobe as they crossed over the bridges. Beneath them, stubborn gondoliers plied their diminished winter trade while the dark gray waters rose past the steps and banks and back entrances to the houses, Venice being reclaimed by the sea as winds reclaimed earth art, though in Gerd's opinion the last could not take place quickly enough.

Skye carried with her a carton of Perugina chocolate sauce with the attachment Stephen Dedalus tendered his ashplant. Chocolate was her secret, deep addiction, her greatest fleshly passion after Gerd. She would go on long ascetic bouts of salad and juices so when the craving came over her, or when she found good chocolate, she could eat as much as she wanted. Perugina was as good a chocolate as any she'd tasted, the chocolate of chocolates. She had never had it as a sauce before and ordered a container to take along with her, to dip into in the night when Gerd couldn't see her. It made her feel guilty, as anything self-indulgent made her feel guilty. Her family gave rise to voluptuaries no more than they did Democrats. Appetites whether for food or social justice were something you didn't show. That she had had the courage to express herself politically, voting the liberal ticket, was rebellion enough. The chocolate, for the most part, she still devoured in secret.

As they walked, she eased the lid from the sauce, sneaking her fingertip inside it. As though in deep thought, she brought her hand up to her mouth, on the side away from him, licking the sweet darkness from her nail without, she thought, his seeing.

"I'll have some of that," he said when they were almost to their hotel. He took her in his arms, right there in the middle of the street with the clouds and the people and the rooftop Madonnas watching, washing the residue of the chocolate from the corner of her mouth with his kiss, seeking the remnants of flavor on her tongue.

They hurried back to the hotel, holding their heat in impatient check till they reached the creaking self-service elevator with its ancient metal gate. He did not release her when the doors ground open but kept his mouth against hers as they moved down the hall, nearly tripping in their rush to get to their room. He unlocked the door while with the other hand he began to loosen her clothes.

"Let me," she said when they were inside, the door shut tight behind them. She began taking off her clothes and his, pulling up his cashmere sweater, tearing at the garments that covered her own body, fingers clumsy at opening his belt, unzipping his jeans.

When they were both naked he asked her what she'd done with the chocolate. She handed him the carton. He took her hand and led her into the bathroom, the one show of grandeur in the place, its great sunken marble tub nearly the size of their bed. He held her by the fingertips, a footman helping a lady descend from her coach. She stepped into the bathtub. He followed. And then he dipped his hands into the chocolate, painted her nipples with it, trailing it down her belly to her mons, rubbing the stickiness from his fingers into the mat of her pubic hair. He bent and started licking it off, sucking it from her breasts, seeking his way with lips and teeth and tongue slowly down the trail he had blazed with his fingers. And then he was kneeling at her naked feet, his chin between her legs, tongue in her hair, cleansing the syrup from her, strand by strand.

"My turn," she said, the longing so intense she could no longer keep her hands to herself. He got to his feet and like a child obediently held out the open carton. She dripped chocolate up onto his lips, strained with her mouth for his mouth while her hands slowly coated his penis, traced syrup down over his balls. She was on her knees, easing his legs apart, licking his testes. She moved her ministrations up to his penis, savoring it like the Good Humors of her youth, flashing her tongue up and down the length of it, working the chocolate off before giving herself to the underlying flavor, plunging the whole of him inside her lips, tensing her tongue away from the roof of her mouth so there was room for passage into her throat. He moaned, and she could feel his spasms inside her cheeks. The flavor of salt mixed with the sweetness. She swallowed the two tastes together before letting him go.

They washed each other, soaped each other, standing, the waters of the tub rising as they washed. They sat down in the liquid warmth and shampooed each other's hair with fragrant shampoos she had brought along to transform anyplace they were to the Gritti Palace. And he was ready again, taking her across his slippery thighs, spearing her, sliding backwards into the water. They were laughing and splashing and drowning and coming all at the same time, with the water around them, underneath them, inside them.

They dried each other with rough grainy towels, lay for a while in each other's arms on the bed, watching night descend on the rooftops outside the window. They felt hungry, so they dressed and went downstairs to the dark little cave next to the street, La Caravella, decorated like an eighteenth-century Spanish galleon, with red and beige banquettes along the wood-paneled walls, ropes and tarnished brass fittings, captain's chairs and gas lamps. They ordered crêpes certosini, creamy with mushrooms and rich white sauce inside the delicate paste.

"And you don't believe in destiny," she said, closing her eyes, tasting. "We just happen to fall into the best restaurant in all of Venice, right in this hotel. And you don't think we're guided."

"I never said that."

He looked at her in the candlelight. She caught her reflection in the mirror on the wall and wondered if her skin had the glow it seemed to or if it was just seeing herself so close to him that made her look golden. She reached for his hand.

"Don't touch me for a while," he said. She could feel her expression change to that of a disappointed child, see the hurt reflected.

"That doesn't mean I don't like it," he said. "It only means I want to think of something besides making love to you, for a few minutes at least."

"That sounds reasonable."

"I am always reasonable."

"*Too* reasonable."

"A man can't be an artist and be *too* reasonable." He

111

reached over and touched her hair.

She closed her eyes, turned her face so her cheek rested against the inside of his palm. "I wish I could tell you not to touch me," she said.

"I wouldn't listen."

Candles flickered darkly inside multicolored bubble-glass lanterns. Outside, claps of thunder sounded. The waiter hovered near the table, bringing fresh bread, fussing, pouring wine. Skye held back a giggle at how attentive he was.

"He likes looking at you," Gerd said when the man had finally gone.

"He likes looking at *us.*" She moved her eyes away from his face so she could say it. "We look like we're in love."

"Appearances can be deceiving," he said.

But back in the room there were no appearances to be deceiving. They were in the dark. So there was only touch between them, and smell. She lay with her head on his smooth, flat belly, her fingers resting on the hollow above his pelvic bone, taking in the clean fragrance of him.

The sky was suddenly ripped with lightning, consecutive flashes illuminating the air outside more clearly than if it were day. Thunder sounded so close and loud it literally made the room tremble. Through the vine-wrapped railings of their balcony she could see the rooftops of Venice flashing as if in a psychedelic light show. Over the gardens, planted next to the sky, past chimneys and turrets glinted the brilliant white marble frieze of a church, cherubs, rococo angels and Madonna cowering inside its angles as though fearing the storm.

They could feel the electricity move into them. She was on him, straddling him, her buttocks toward his waist, thrusting the hard length of him inside her. His warm hands pressed against her back, rocked her.

112

And she rode him through the storm, shuddering with the thunder. While outside the window, the marble angels wept in a torrent of rain.

AND THAT, as she had described it to me in such detail, was what she was trying to recapture, that was the magic she hoped to retrieve, when she threw up on his shoes. My pity was equaled only by my wonder at the terrible sense of comedy displayed by the universe, the mocking laughter of the gods, who, we assume, take life as seriously as we do.

"AM I dead?" Skye asked me the morning after, pulling the covers away from her face.

"I don't think so."

She pulled them up again.

"You better comb your hair before he sees you."

"Who?" The covers moved down a little, enough to show one eye.

"Gerd. He's on the patio."

"He is?" She sat up sharply, her face lit with happiness, until she remembered. "How can I face him?"

"Well, you can't till you brush your hair."

She got out of bed, staggered to the bathroom, still obviously woozy from her overdose. I could hear the racket of the plumbing, the deep hollow echoes that sound in the pipes of European castles even when they masquerade as modern villas. Having arrived with four rolls of toilet paper, which Customs had opened and examined, I had been pleasantly surprised to discover that that facet of European convenience had nearly caught up with ours and that the French no longer have to wipe their bottoms with sandpaper. It would have been too much to hope that their sanitary facilities had made the same leap. It was enough that it was a civilization that had given rise to croissants, and where the *Herald Tribune* was still available.

Skye came out looking pale beneath what was left of her tan, easing into something white and flowing, nearly transparent, a number Marguerite Gautier might have worn just before fainting into Armand's arms. "I can't let him see me," she said, examining herself in front of the mirror, slipping off her underpants.

"Of course you can. You can and must," I said stubbornly, as if I believed she really meant what she was saying. "He was here five times yesterday. He's really concerned about you."

She looked at me with that combination of hope and disbelief that seems to characterize the twentieth century. Most of us thinking that the best could happen but is unlikely, waiting at the curb for the Rolls-Royce of Faith, settling for a Toyota.

"He made me promise to call him the minute you came to. Charlotte answered the phone." I swallowed, feeling my throat close the way it had when I heard her voice. I walked to the window and looked down at the Mittri swimming pool. Someone was splashing on his back, doing slow strokes the length of it. It looked like the Yorky, a flesh-colored rubber cap pulled over the right side of his face, covering his wound. Otherwise he was completely exposed. Something long and thin and pink floated between his legs, and I wondered if he wouldn't be safer putting a protective cap on that too. Sometimes, there were sharks in unexpected places.

"Why are you afraid of Charlotte?" Skye asked me.

"She makes me nervous," I said, again pulling back from the

impulse to tell her to be careful because I sensed a shadow looming behind us.

"Tell Gerd I'm sorry," Skye instructed, putting on her lipstick. "But I can't possibly see him."

"Stop being a child," I said, playing along. "He's out there alone."

"Artists have to be alone or they can't be artists," she said, as though quoting a long-ago dictum he had issued to her. She reached into the bodice of her negligee, slightly adjusting her breasts so that each nipple appeared symmetrically in the center of a panel of the chiffony fabric and stepped back from the mirror. "I won't see him." She slid open the glass door to the patio, stepped outside, stepped back, and said softly, "Come with me."

"I don't belong there."

"Did that really happen the other night? I didn't dream it?"

I shook my head.

"Oh, God." She held onto the wall, cooling her face against it. "How can I face him?"

"You'll be missing something if you don't."

"I didn't dream that either, then? He's handsomer than he was?"

I nodded.

"Damn him," she said. "Tess, please, stay here. I need to know you're here," and she was outside before I could protest.

I went to the door, leaned back against the wall, and watched her move toward him. The day had decked itself out as gingerly as Skye had arranged her breasts. Gerd sat on a rock just beneath a silver-leafed olive tree near a cluster of oaks, slender maritime pine towering over all like great green cumulus clouds crowning the scene. Of actual clouds there were none. In the distance, tall pointed peaks of cypress marked the road to the sea. Beyond one roundly verdant hill sparkled that sea itself, spotted with colored sails and white-painted yachts on their way back to harbor.

Which Skye seemed to be too. But like a sailor too long at sea, no longer sure of the shoreline, she hung back slightly. Gerd stood. I could see the composure slip from her bearing as she looked up into his face.

He was wearing a V-necked yellow sweater. It looked soft, clinging to the lean line of his torso, the slimness of his waist accentuated by the width of his shoulders, deep gold chest hair showing over the ribbing of the V. "How have you been?" he asked formally.

"Awful," she said.

"Why must you be so honest? Can't you learn to hold back?"

"It wasn't because of you," she said quickly. "I'm over loving you." She would force herself to say what he wanted to hear.

"You promised in the beginning you weren't going to love me. That was the agreement."

"I lied."

"So how do I know you're not lying now, when you say you don't love me anymore?"

"You don't," she said, and smiled.

He sat down on the rock and patted the flat place beside him. She stayed standing. He reached over and put his finger casually inside the fold of chiffon at her breasts, tracing the round contour inside.

"You're looking very beautiful." He kissed her throat. I could see her tremble. She struggled to stay balanced, to avoid falling against him.

He held her off a little, and touched her hair. "What a woman you would be if you'd only learn to think like a man."

"How does a man think?"

"Not to surrender. Not to be devoured. Women want to be a part of something else, a man, a family, to be swallowed."

"Don't you want to be a part of anything?"

"History," he said. "Art."

"What a man you would be if you only had an ego."

He laughed. "That's what you love most—"

"Not anymore."

"Swear it."

"I swear."

His hands moved up the backs of her legs, folds of chiffon clustering about his fingers. "If only I could believe you," he said. "What an affair we could have."

"Believe me." She was trying too hard to sound convincing about it, but I could hear the pleading.

"No." His hands were on her naked buttocks, and rested there. "You'd fall in love with me again, and spoil it."

"I couldn't."

"No?" His heavy eyebrows raised, eyes focused on her lips.

"It was shot off in the war," she said. "My love for you. I have a letter from my doctor."

He laughed. He took her lovely chin between his hands and studied her face with a look so deep, so sunlit, so liquid, it made one understand why, in spite of all the differences, there are two sexes. "Swear?" he said.

"I swear."

"Liar."

And then they kissed, their mouths moving, all over each other.

I LEFT then, my assignment over, and drove down the hill and along the curving road to Les Bergerettes, where without much ado I wrapped myself around Sal. As much as I was moved by the passion between Skye and Gerd, I enjoyed it more for myself. As Sal did too, although he did listen interestedly when I told him afterwards about Skye's reunion with Gerd and the history of their grand amour, though leaving out all the carnality she had confided, transmuting it into certain actions of my own.

EARLY THE next afternoon I returned to find Skye's house frenzied with activity. Servants I had never seen before were polishing the white terrazzoed floors, vacuuming the furniture and the drapes. A piano tuner worked listlessly on the white-painted piano that seemed to have been placed there largely for decor, its keyboard warped by the nearness of the ocean and seeming decades of neglect. In the kitchen, the stove had all its burners going, low flames heating a *roux* for sauces, sorrel soup simmering, a great pot of water coming to a boil. It was all being watched carefully by a nervous young maid in uniform who kept going over to a blackboard on which Skye had scrawled instructions alongside the dinner menu. The author of all this organized confusion was nowhere to be found. I assumed from the look and busyness of it all that there was to be a huge dinner party. But I found a note on my bed inviting me and Sal to join Skye and another guest for dinner at nine. From the devotional atmosphere of the preparations I had no doubt about the fourth guest's identity.

About three, she came back from the village, her arms filled with flowers, only a little less resplendent and blooming than her face. She was followed by her valet, who was likewise floridly encumbered, the bottom half of his body visible beneath radiant purple blossoms. He made three more trips down the steps, and two more into the village, for ficus trees and rhododendrons in fuchsias and pinks. By four o'clock the sterile white room was transformed to a greenhouse, missing only the glass walls.

Skye draped leftover fabrics from the other day's fashion invasion around the pots in which the plants grew so that everything gave the illusion of planned decor. The huge crystal chandelier that dangled Harlowesquely above the conversation pit was reoutfitted with soft pink candlebulbs, so when night fell the room would have the same understated glow she did.

The dining alcove was off to the side of the living room, its table set with the finest linen, which she'd bought that day. Fresh flowers were arranged in bud vases in front of each place, a tall, slender taper in the middle of each. The centerpiece would be laid that evening, but she unveiled it for my imagination: there between green-leafed branches cut from her garden would be interwoven fresh yellow roses, yellow daisies and ferns lying at the base of three candlesticks of Jensen Royal Danish, the silver she had brought with her from home, just in case, part of the trousseau she had carefully collected but never used.

All was in readiness, or nearly all. Tortellini, homemade, hand-rolled, was lying on the sideboard to be plunged into the water. The duckling was already in the oven, heat lower than traditional recipes dictated—a trick she had learned from a chef at Cordon Bleu—to drain the fat and slowly crisp the skin. Only the piano gave her concern. After several hours of tuning it was still off-key. She raced back to the village, and reported back a short while later with unprecedented exuberance that she had found a folk harpist on the dock in front of *Senequier* to substitute for the pianist she'd planned on having.

"A harpist!" she said. "Won't that be medieval and lovely? We'll be ladies and knights."

"In shining armor?" I asked, a kind of sorrow building in my heart because I saw how she was, and where it was probably leading, again. And because I, really, was not much smarter, trying to make history where there was only heat. Because none of us, really, knew just how to have dinner.

"Well, maybe a little rusty," she said. I thought I could hear doom ticking, like the antique clock on the mantel with its gilded Louis Quinze face.

SAL ARRIVED at the stroke of nine, wearing a sports jacket and tie. I had never seen him rigged as a gentleman before, and in a funny way it touched me. Gerd got there a few minutes later, in a cream-colored shirt open at the collar, white pants and a dark blue blazer with a crest on the pocket, as if he had come directly from Charlotte's yacht or a photo layout session with GQ. I do not mean to imply that he was superficial, merely that he looked good enough to be superficial.

He seemed annoyed at the presence of Sal. "You didn't tell me it would be a party," he said to Skye.

"It's just the four of us," she said.

"And thirty-seven in help," I added, taking a piece of celery from the *crudité* tray to cover my nervousness.

"Sal Boglio," Sal said, getting to his feet, extending his hand. Gerd took it. "Mittri. Gerd Mittri."

"I'm a longtime admirer of yours," Sal said.

"You know painting?"

"I know good stuff," Sal said.

"Stuff," said Gerd, appraising the word, as though it were in a gallery, and went to pour himself a drink.

120

It is easy to tell when two men don't like each other. And with those two it was apparent from the moment they met, as if someone had said, "Shake hands and come out fighting." It was particularly hard for me, because I knew how important the evening was to Skye, but I preferred the one in the striped trunks. (In a fit of tender curiosity I had looked in Sal's dresser drawers and made a quick study of his underwear.)

Sal reached for a paper-wrapped bundle on the chair beside him and handed it to Skye. "These are for you."

"How lovely," she said, unwrapping. She was dressed in violet hostess pajamas that pulled all the colors of the flowers and the fabrics in the room together. "Daisies, my favorite."

"I thought your favorite was roses," said Gerd, ice clinking against his glass as he stirred, his back to us.

"Then maybe you should have brought her some," I couldn't help saying, already knowing whose second I was.

To the side of the alcove the folk harpist played, her voice tiny and serene, lilting over the melody like hindsight. She wore a medieval costume, tight below the breast, braided with gold. Her fingers were long and white and slim, plucking melancholy from the strings of the ancient instrument leaning up against her. Regrettably, her selection was "Greensleeves," and her love was just at the point of casting her off discourteously. It seemed a little too apt, especially as she bore a ghostly resemblance to Skye, except that her hair was long and trailing in its gold, her face older, as though the sorrows of the songs she sang were personal experience.

We had drinks. Everyone struggled for amiability, with the exception of Gerd, who seemed inordinately prickly, looking forward to the joust.

In left-handed fashion he complimented Skye on the beauty of her table as we sat down. "How many flowers had to die to give such grace to your table?"

"Flowers don't mind dying in the process of giving beauty," she said.

"Like women," Gerd said.

"You don't like women?" Sal asked.

"Not usually," Gerd said. "But sometimes I love them."

"I don't think it's possible to love without liking." Sal sat very straight, the soft camel color of his jacket serving to make more intense the brown of his eyes.

"Are you gay?" Gerd asked him.

"Are you?"

"I am always suspicious of people who answer a question with a question."

"Then maybe you ought to ask better questions," said Sal.

"All right. What brought you to the South of France?"

"An airplane," Sal said.

"A true wit," said Gerd. "Are you sure you're not gay?"

"This is incredible soup," I interjected, seeing the anxiety on Skye's face. "Sorrel is so . . . sassy."

"Sorrel is so sassy?" Gerd repeated with disdain, the acid he felt for Sal etching its way toward me, the culprit who had brought him. "Sorrel is so *sassy?*"

"It's the sharp edge," I continued, panicked. "France has always prized it as an invigorating herb, but Americans traditionally aren't partial to bitter flavors—"

"What in God's name is she talking about?" Gerd asked.

"Tess is a food writer," Skye told him.

"A *food* writer. That must be like being in a symphony orchestra and playing the triangle."

At this moment, something quite peculiar occurred. From the time it had ended with me and Elliott I had been constitutionally incapable of talking about it, with tics pulling at my mouth when the subject came up, kind of choking around the word *divorce,* an actual breaking up of words in my throat when I tried to speak glibly or casually of what had happened, as if some kind of static or interference were being sent out from a relay station, cutting off the news, like a spy in World War II. Being a subscriber to Psychology Today, and a resident of San Francisco, a certain amount of enlightenment would have had to have taken place even if I were thick, so I understood perfectly well that it was a dulling, an anesthesia against the pain, a kind of self-censorship or, as it were, nature's way of telling me to shut up. I assumed that the area under siege was simply the marriage zone; shock at my failure to preserve, letting the flag drag on the ground, etc. That selfsame Psychology Today had informed me that marriage was becoming more or less obsolete, less only when the wives had traditional jobs like secretaries and waitresses. Had I but limited my quest to Howard Johnson's, with Simple Simon meeting the Pieman across my breast, would he have continued to fondle it?

But suddenly there, in the midst of that awkwardly antagonistic dinner, my voice disappeared completely. I tried to parry Gerd's thrust with a witty riposte and nothing came out but air. I must have tried ten different sentences at least, some that bore no relation to my situation, just sharp little jibes I had prepared in case I ever ran into Gore Vidal. There was no sound.

I sipped some water to cover my paroxysm.

"Are you all right?" Skye said.

I nodded my head. There was no point in adding to her anguish and discomfort at how agley these best-laid plans had gone. How much easier would it have been for the ancient sages to suffer in silence, had they had the benefit of aphonia, which, I was to discover the next day, was the medical terminology for my ailment.

"You have the tact of Godzilla," Sal told Gerd.

"I just calls 'em like I sees em, as the umpire said." Gerd smiled. "And what did *you* say you did?"

"I didn't," Sal answered as Skye rang the little silver bell in front of her, like a referee signaling the end of the round. The soup was cleared, the plates changed, the duckling served. I cannot detail what it tasted like, since flavor and memory seemed also to have left me.

I must confess that besides having literally rendered me speechless, Gerd seemed to be inflicting some damage on himself. His face darkened with each course, as if he were cooking his own spleen while dishing it out. The reason for his rancor was a mystery to me, one I knew I would better be able to ferret out when I was not so caught up in my own discomfort. Something was obviously eating at him. I wondered if it was the combination of having Nazis nipping at his ass in childhood and critics nipping at his heels in recent years, annoyed with him for his popularity and the prices he commanded. Or maybe his mother hadn't loved him, but only justice and freedom. Maybe his father had been so busy resisting tyrants he hadn't bounced him on his knee. Maybe the struggle he had gone through to achieve had worn him out by the time success finally came. Or maybe he was just an asshole.

"How long will you be visiting Saint-Tropez?" Gerd asked Sal.

"I don't know. Till my business is finished I suppose."

"What business is that?"

"I'm here to design a security system for the museum."

"A security system," Gerd said. "Is that what you do in the States?"

"That's right."

"I would have thought our little *musée* would be too poor to afford a hotshot American—"

"I'm not a hotshot."

"You heard it from his own lips," Gerd said to me, resting his case.

"How did you happen to get into the security business?" Skye asked interestedly.

"My dad was with the CIA," he said.

"What a heritage. Do they pass that down?" Gerd said. "Like making cuckoo clocks in Switzerland?"

"They do, if you're interested."

"And were you?"

"I studied to be a psychologist," said Sal, his voice even.

"How boring." Gerd drank some wine.

"I don't know, I could probably be a big help to you."

"As a therapist, or a burglar alarm?"

Skye rang the bell for dessert.

"Well, what a gathering you've managed, Skye," Gerd said. "The Elizabeth Barrett Browning of Lutèce, and Freud of the CIA."

There's a moment among the best of the best-bred when, perhaps because of their breeding, they ignore etiquette and show true class. "I regret," said Skye, "that it could not be as riveting as what you have below. Your harridan and her refugee from Harrow."

"Adam?" He looked at her curiously. "You've seen Adam?"

"Seen him and heard him. Belittling you in public. In English and French."

"Well, he's a gifted boy. He has a quick ear."

"My God, you can't have grown so calloused. Not about yourself. Have you no pride?"

"Only in my work. My marriage is not important."

"Then why did you do it?"

He was silent. The dessert came. We all pretended we could taste it.

"I see he's living with you now, this Adam," Skye continued. The singer with her sweetly mournful voice sang of devotion misplaced.

"He's suffered some injury . . . to his feelings," Gerd said. "It's cheaper to take him in than have a lawsuit."

"What does he want with her?" Skye asked.

"Maybe he misses his mommy." Gerd shrugged.

"And what do you miss?"

"I miss your devotional silences, when your beauty was enough to carry any gathering. I miss the young woman I loved because she wanted nothing from me, including answers to pointless questions."

"Excuse me," said Skye and left the table.

"You're a real shit, you know that?" Sal said.

"As a trained psychologist, Mr. Boglio, I would venture that you are incapable of distinguishing between real shit, and *phony* shit."

Sal got to his feet and moved to the other side of the table. "Get up."

Gerd held his hands up in front of his chest, palms out and open. "I won't fight you. My hands . . ."

"You coward prick bastard—"

"Wrong again. I'm not a coward. But I pick the time. And choice of weapons."

"Name it," Sal said.

"I'll let you know when I'm ready."

By this time I had gotten to my own feet, and wedged my body, which I could still move around on its legs, between the two men, thinking less to protect my protector than ensure that he would not ruin the summer for Skye. I was convinced that Sal could tear Gerd apart, wiry little Sicilian that he now appeared to me to be, bursting with honor, and maybe Mafia connections. I couldn't accept what he'd dropped on the table as truth, that his father was CIA, since I expected cloaks to obscure even familial pride in that area. So, I figured, ashamed to admit that his dad was a member of the Mafia, he'd turned it around and fantasized him into CIA.

"Sit down, Mimi Sheraton," Gerd said.

"Save your poison for your own women," Sal warned him.

"Poison?" Gerd smiled. "That's how much you know. Skye's never been happier."

Did he know her that much better than the rest of us?

I went into Skye's bedroom. To my astonishment, she was sitting quite calmly in front of her dressing table, brushing her hair. She looked at me in the mirror, panic momentarily crossing her face.

"Did he leave?"

I shook my head.

A smile flashed across her face. "Then let's go back and have coffee," she said.

SIX

It was a fancy of mine once, before Mittri's attack on me, when I still believed food could be lifted through words to a higher significance, to give a dinner party with seven courses based on the Seven Deadly Sins. For the first one, Pride, I intended to serve little birds, with brittle bones, whose final act before being rotisseried had been crowing. For Anger, I planned a jellied madrilene, laced with chopped hot chili peppers to effect being burned inside even while experiencing something cold—in my view, a perfect metaphor for what anger feels like and does to you. Covetousness gave me a few problems: I settled finally on quenelles, to be eaten off someone else's plate. Lust was a puffed potato, devoured in a single mouthful; Gluttony, an outsized slab of roast beef rare, still on the rib. Envy was a salad; it worked for color (green) and representationally, since what we usually envy others for is their

129

"lettuce." Sloth was a chocolate mousse, in which anyone worth their own potential decadence can visualize themselves vanishing forever, usually upside down.

But with the dinner party at Skye's, I experienced an instantaneous revisionistic view of Sin, and with it my dinner menu. And those were that there is only one Sin, incorporating all Seven, and that is Cruelty, and what it is is a Meat Loaf.

To keep the evening less painful than it already was, I did not make known to anyone what had happened to my voice. The occasion had not existed in previous experience, outside of a concert or a play, where I had been quiet for long. In one of my high schools the housemother accused me of having "mental diarrhea," to which I responded, accurately if maybe a little too high on my hind legs, that if it were mental, she wouldn't know about it, and what she meant, I believed, was "oral diarrhea." She campused me for the weekend and went on to become the warden in a female prison. The truth. But no one at the dinner party knew me well enough to realize my behavior was atypical, except Skye, who was too caught up in making the evening work for the Mengele of the art world to notice.

Although presumedly less schooled in my psychology than Sal, I understood clearly what had happened. My life, my identity, had been at that moment vaporized. It was not simply hurt that wound its way around my vocal cords but annihilation. Lost now was not only my certainty about myself as a woman woman, but also as a working woman, that road only recently opened to the average female as an alternate route to heaven, or, at least, the Emerald City of Survival. The yellow brick road lay wrecked beneath my feet, petty and acrid, sewer pipes exposed.

Sprung as I was from the brainpan of my mother, I'd first

considered my continuity depended on the good will of my husband. Seeing that turn before my eyes to good bob, good hank, etc., I had gone through an emergency change in gears and pinned my hopes on my career. I knew that in the cold, cruel world (although granted, in San Francisco, it is never worse than chilly and impolite) anyone could be replaced, especially women. Orthodox feminist that I am not, I nonetheless sympathize with and accept the truths, that women earn only fifty-nine cents to the man's dollar, that if present trends of limited jobs, divorce rates and weak economy continue, by the turn of the century nearly all the nation's poor will be women and children. Having never aggrandized what I did, I still never felt contempt for myself, until Mittri said what he did at dinner and carved out what small core of self-esteem I had, without anesthesia and with a dull knife. It is the most amazing characteristic of women that their self-image can be obliterated by a man for whom they have no real respect.

I went with Sal back to Les Bergerettes because I did not want to sleep, suspected I couldn't sleep under the same roof where my tormentor was popping Skye, especially as I now knew so much intimate detail about them. There was a rage in me, a sense of violation, because she loved him as much as she did, because, whatever else, he was as gifted as he was, as accomplished, as invulnerable, as good in bed. There was no way I could make my dislike and discomfort known to her without risking losing her as a friend. Once I had told my mother how little I thought of one of her suitors, certain that my influence as her daughter would surely outstrip any he had, only to find myself on my way to sleepaway school.

Sal did not realize the extent of my wound. Not knowing me well enough to recognize I was incapable of keeping still, he imagined I was merely brooding over the incident and not that my voice box didn't work. I considered writing him a note on the small pad at his bedside, but before I could, his hands and lips were on me, and I threw myself completely into the experience of making love as a mute, at one point imagining myself being raped and unable to cry out, which doubtless would offend the women's movement, but I found very hot.

I felt Garboesque and mysterious, in that quiet concupiscence, fascinating to myself as I realized for the first time the power of silence. Not having to say things like "touch me there," because he did, and very well too. Even in that heart-tugging moment afterwards, when I had had such a battle not to say "I love you," and had settled for thanks, I noticed how much deeper the whole experience went for not being orchestrated with words. Words had always been my best suit, or so I had thought. Now there was a certain dark majesty to every moment because I could not damage it by asking too much.

We slept in each other's arms, my nose drunk with the musky scent coming from the warm, dark place in his armpit. His fingers were caught in the curl of my hair. It seemed very affectionate, but I couldn't spoil it by saying, "Are you starting to care about me?" My eyes felt very wide in the darkness, clear, touching, searching, like Jane Wyman's in *Johnny Belinda*, which Elliott and I used to watch every time it was on television, moving as it was, and controversial, sparking the discussing of whether or not she was sorry she had let Ronald Reagan go. There was a certain modest sweetness Belinda had that I struggled to incorporate into my character as I lay there, wakeful, trying to sort out the difference between humility and humiliation.

With dawn, I experienced panic. I went into Sal's bathroom, closed the door and performed my ablutions with a fair amount of attempted noise, gargling. Bubbles rose in my throat, but no sound. I spit out the minty solution, told myself "good morning" in the mirror. Nothing came out except a little pop of air.

I dressed in the jeans I'd changed into before leaving Skye's villa and went for a walk in the woods behind the hotel. There were foot-pressed paths in between the tall pines, gorse bushes and heather, slightly defined trails down the gently rolling hills to the main road below. I tried to sing, snuck up on myself with a casual salute to the burgeoning nature around me. Nothing. I tried to scream. The birds seemed unimpressed, staring at me, silent, beady-eyed.

Sal was breakfasting on the balcony terrace outside his room when I came out of the woods. The air was already warm, although the sun was not yet visible, except as a sheaf of orange across the sea. "Good morning," he said, his wide, white smile a balm to my spirit if not my larynx.

"I've lost my voice," I pantomimed.

He signaled me upstairs, poured me some tea, sweetened it with honey, pressed it to my lips. Pressed his own lips on mine, a sure sign of genuine regard, I thought, since he couldn't be sure it wasn't an infection. "Can you make any sound at all?" he asked.

I shook my head. To show him, I tried. A lark sang in a nearby vineyard, its voice sweetened with grapes. But no sound came out of my throat.

THE DOCTOR at the clinic on the main road, speaking excellent English, told us what it was was hysterical aphonia. There was nothing wrong with the nerves, nothing organic in my throat. He asked if I'd had some shock, something that frightened me. Sal told the doctor I'd been insulted.

"It must have been a very grave insult," the doctor said.

He assured us that the condition would go away by itself when the conditions that brought it on went away, or when I had another shock. At this point he took Sal off to the side and talked to him in muted tones.

THERE ARE some places eminently suited to a mute. First among them I would place museums, which is where Sal took me that morning, seeking to combine business, pleasure, aesthetic longings and dumbness. The Musée de l'Annonciade, from which he had received his commission to install a security system, was a graystoned two-story building just next to the port, footsteps away from the stylish madness of the Gorilla Cafe, where those who had only recently fallen out of the doors of the all-night discos were devouring their morning croissants. Red-eyed, and glittering, sparkles on their lashes and some on their clothes, as if the mirrored walls and ceilings of the private clubs had shattered around them, they more or less faced the day. A number of them were wearing distressed leather, chamois that had been beaten past death, and overdyed.

The museum was not yet open to the public, but the guard obviously knew Sal, unchained the great iron gate to the courtyard, then unlocked the museum's double doors. I was touched by the serious attempt at grandeur of the entry hall, combining marble floors with a little wooden desk behind which, Sal explained, ladies would later sit and collect an eight-franc entry fee.

The museum itself was deceptively deep—it had seemed quite small from outside—going back through several high-ceilinged rooms complete with marble columns, huge canvases of no great distinction, there being on display at the time an exhibition entitled "Fleurs," with which, in my opinion, only

Fantin-Latour had done anything riveting, and none of those were represented. On the rear wall of the third and most cavernous room was a gigantic painting, gilt-framed, of oversized sunflowers from the center of which rose Mary, Queen of Heaven, in a style that I think might have given even her forgiveness pause.

But on the second floor, up a circular stairway, along the landings of which hung some minor masterpieces, was as fine a collection of paintings as could be found in a provincial museum. While Sal scurried into corners, checking windows, examining skylights, I made my own leisurely tour. And I could not help but note, in the strange new awareness awakening in me, that there among the Raouls (Dufy), Pierres (Bonnard), Henris (Matisse), Kees (van Dongen), there was only one Suzanne, and she a Valadon, who'd died in 1938. Why, I wondered, had not more women painted, since that was something they could do in secret, in silence, without confronting their societies? Art was a gift, as writing was, yet there had been many women who wrote. Why were there not more painters? Had the gods reserved those kisses for the men? Or was the truth, perhaps, that women were too busy with the tasks assigned to them, weaving, sewing, cooking, making the men comfortable so they could better express themselves. Was it even a more devious truth than that? Could it have been that women who demonstrated talent were absorbed by their partners, as Colette had been, handcuffed to the bedstead by her husband, forced to write, with his publishing her works under his name. Could it be it was really (Irene) Dufy, (Paulette) Bonnard, (Marguerite) Matisse, (Anjanette) van Dongen?

My musings were interrupted by a rude pinch to my right nipple, which did not frighten so much as annoy me, since I had felt Sal sneaking up on me and expected a kiss, or gentle

135

touch, as was his style. It apparently upset him too, as he seemed constrained to explain that the doctor had suggested that only by some unexpected and sudden physical thrust, as it were, that might startle me and not give me time to censor my own sound, not give me the opportunity to get my defenses up, might my voice be restored. It had not worked at this moment. But both moving, as I seemed to be, into greater consciousness of my plight as a woman and backsliding into the latent masochism of my sex, I confess I looked forward to whatever would be his next assault.

MEANWHILE IN another more publicized citadel of the art world, Saint-Paul-de-Vence, another appreciation was about to occur. Skye was later to tell me what transpired without, I am frankly relieved to say, a great deal of prurient detail. She did, however, again demonstrate her astonishing recall by reciting verbatim the dialogue, which I set down here. It is through people's words that we best know them, since in spite of the homily, actions do not speak louder. And I want to examine the conversation, myself, to see if it contained any portent of the misfortunes that were later to take place.

As ANYONE can tell you who has ever tried to avoid anyone, there are only twenty-five people in the world, and eight places. So no matter how discreet you try to be you are always going to come face to face with the very person you are trying to steer clear of, usually in the middle of the place you go to elude them. I knew a woman who was caught up in an adulterous affair—not the kind they have in France, where it is as common as a fish course—but one that was giving her a great deal

of pain, since she deeply loved her husband but was patheti-
cally drawn to a silly man. She chose the most déclassé hotel
in California to meet with him, one that would be frequented
by no one either of them knew, and ran smack into her sister,
who was supposed to be on a commune in Taos. In the same
way, if you go to church to ask for forgiveness for not wanting
to see your mother, your mother will have that same day redis-
covered God, and sit in the next pew.

Although it was a stringent discipline of Gerd's never to
socialize in the daytime, Skye had set her heart on a short trip
to Saint-Paul-de-Vence, a village in the Maritime Alps. Built
into the side of a mountain, the town featured what is regarded
as one of France's finest restaurants, La Colombe d'Or. It was
there that artists later to become renowned gave paintings to
the management in exchange for meals, which art is still displayed in the lobby of the hotel—Matisse, Calder, Léger, and
César struggling to brighten up the cold, raw silk-covered stone
walls.

The restaurant adorned a red-bricked patio shaded with
beige-and-brown umbrellas set among fig trees and huge pots
of flowering fuchsias and red geraniums. Across the deep valley
adjacent was another, slightly higher hill, terraced with gray
rock and greenhouses, glass windowpanes reflecting silver in
the bright glare of day. It was Skye's favorite place in all of
France, next to Paris. Her late psychiatrist had once told her
that green was the color that best soothed the spirit. Green was
all you saw from the terrace of La Colombe d'Or, infinite
varieties of green, palest ocher, malachite, absinthe, silvery
green olive trees along the ridge making shadows, leaves waving
in a gentle wind like handkerchiefs signaling kisses to a faraway
love.

Across the cobblestoned street from the hotel and restaurant, shops sold the herbs of Provence, rosemary, marjoram, summer savory and thyme, aromas overflowing the woven baskets in which they were displayed, drifting through the streets, overwhelming the fragrance of fresh-cut flowers on the restaurant tables. Skye rejoiced in the scents, taking them in with immoderate gusto, all the zest that Gerd seemed unable to show. Why, she really wasn't sure. It was as if he had gone through some crisis of spirit since Italy, turning him liverish, like the dark reds and grays and blues of his paintings. She did not love him less because he had changed, could not censure him for being different, like a critic reviewing pigment on canvas. Love was not love when it judged.

Besides, just because he showed no enthusiasm for the journey didn't take away from the fact that he had made it. She understood what a surrender it had been for him, he who was so inflexible in his commitment to work, so disciplined in the hours he set for his painting. To have left his fortress in the daylight hours was abandon enough. They had driven off into the bright middle of day, his little gray two-seater Mercedes convertible raising a cloud of dust wider than the car. And now they sat overlooking the viridescent glow of the valley, their table against an old wooden wall next to a tiny recessed iron door, rusted and latched, through which, Skye imagined, Joan of Arc might have passed the message that saved France.

Beside the bowl of flowers in the center of the pale pink tablecloth was a pepper mill, the same burnished oak as the wall behind them, and a clear salt mill, the crystals inside sparkling like the day. Stemmed wine and water glasses glittered in the sunlight as did the jewels worn by the women, some just off ships cruising to the Aegean, others French dowagers celebrating a place where there was still a special menu and no one wearing distressed clothes. Everyone animated and smiling, except the couple at the table directly next to Gerd and Skye, who, the world being as it is, were Adam and Charlotte.

"Well, well, well," said Charlotte. "What a terrible surprise."

DURING THIS time I had returned to Skye's villa. Sal thought a nap would be good for me, he said. I could see him checking the trellises and balconies even as he seemed to be simply saying good-by. I expected a later, startling and marvelous attack on my person, which I tried to put out of my mind so it would be a surprise.

A little after one, or thirteen hours, the doorbell rang. The maid informed me that there was a gentleman in the living room who wished to speak with me, in the absence of the mistress of the house. I went out to greet him, more ladylike than I have ever been, dumb as I was. One of the things I had begun to notice is that no one takes it amiss when a woman is silent. On the contrary it would seem to be regarded as the correct order of things, accepted more easily than, for instance, her having something to say.

Having been informed by the maid that I didn't speak too much French (*"Americaine,"* she said to him, which explained it *all*), he began to talk to me in a kind of English, part *patois*, part Inspector Clouseau. He bore, in fact, an uncanny resemblance to Peter Sellers, which fortified my belief that talent does not die but is transmuted back to the living, who usually don't know what to do with it, especially comedy. He showed me his credentials: he was a journalist for France *Soir.* His newspaper had received some anonymous rumors about the painter Mittri. He had had no luck below, since neither Gerd

139

nor Charlotte was at home, and the servants had refused to answer his questions. He was making general inquiry about the painter, calling on me simply as a neighbor, not suspecting that I was the house guest of Mittri's (once-again) mistress.

Reporters, if not answered at once, become anxious, like a person going to a psychic who wants so desperately for the psychic to get it right he feeds her a constant nervous stream of facts, and then is astounded by how much she seers. Had I noted anything curious? A strangeness or inconsistency of habits? Was he frequently at home? Had I seen anything of what he was working on now? Did my servants have any relationship with his servants? Could they, for a small consideration, find out what was going on in the Mittri villa, anything that was not—did I understand the expression—kosher?

He took my silence for reticence, and apologized for seeming to pry. Was I familiar with the career of the painter Mittri? I nodded.

"Een nineteen-seventy-two, he receive a Guggenheim Award," he said. "To study in Rome."

I knew about that, of course. That was the idyllic exile to Italy when it had all seemed so blissful to Skye.

"But do anyone check with Guggenheim?" he asked. A dramatic pause. Raising his finger in the air, he answered, "*I* am."

Pride beamed from his face. Investigative reporting in France has, apparently, slumbered since Zola, the Woodwards and Bernsteins of their press being more or less nonexistent, since political corruption is no surprise to anyone there. The way the Gaul bounces. Sorry.

"There is never be a Gerd Mittri received a Guggenheim," he proclaimed.

Then where, if he was right, did the money come from? I

knew he'd paid for their stay in Rome, their trip to Venice. It had been on Skye's account, laying that particular information on me lest I feel any subtle or not so subtle prejudice against him for having abandoned that part of the male responsibility. She had made it clear a number of times. ("We're going to Rome," she'd said, that day, ironing. "Gerd is paying." "We were vacationing in Venice," she'd said, that night in the square when she'd had too much wine. "It was Gerd's treat.") Like a woman who countered suspicions of her man's impotence by telling how often and well they made love, she'd advertised his finally picking up the tab so no one could mark him opportunist.

In the same recounting she had described their days in Italy, less vividly, thank God, than she had their nights. They were rigidly ordered, with Gerd spending the daylight hours at the American Academy or painting in his studio, as he now spent time in the bunker. Except for this sunshiny one, with the two of them off in Saint-Paul-de-Vence, playing vagrant.

Just then a blast of Beethoven echoed up from the hill below, the *Missa Solemnis*. The very trees seemed stunned into respect, as did the reporter. I knew it was a habit of Gerd's to play classical music very loud when he was painting, a kind of self-hypnosis he used to raise his concentration.

The reporter turned. "He is home. They lie." He started back down the steps to his car, and then ran up again, handing me his card. "Call me," he said. "P.C.V."

"En P.C.V.," he urged. "You call, I pay." Then he was gone, apparently without thinking anything odd in my silence. Silence, which Thoreau said, is the communion of the conscious soul with itself. And which, sez I, is the best way of pumping reporters.

I watched him go back to the Mittri villa and assault it, first

141

the bell, and then the servants with gestures so strong I could read them from a distance. He was demanding to be let into the studio. After listening to him with visible restraint the maid shut the door in his face. Undeterred, he went to the iron door of the studio and pounded on it, lifted the huge iron bolt, pressing his full weight against the door. Apparently it was also bolted from the inside. The bunker was windowless white concrete with only a round skylight at the very top. I wondered how a painter could paint, so confined, and wondered too why the music was playing. Probably, I thought, it was a game plan of Mittri's, camouflage the servants had been instructed to put into effect in the event suspicious strangers came.

THE WAITER wheeled a table filled with rectangular white dishes containing *hors-d'oeuvres variés* to the table where Skye and Gerd sat and served them, one by one, spooning them onto Skye's plate. "How are you Charlotte?" she asked, over the waiter's activity.

"Miss Duncan . . ." Charlotte nodded. She was wearing a navy blue straw hat, very wide of brim, parts of it semitransparent, lightly woven so that it appeared like latticework, sending shadows across her once beautiful face, as time had done. "How faithful you are. I would have imagined by now you would have found another great cultural hero to admire, like Joe Namath."

Gerd signaled for the maître d', asking if they could be moved to another table. The maître d' regretted that the restaurant was fully booked.

"Don't be a prig, darling," Charlotte said. "Let's move into the twentieth century and have lunch together."

"No, thank you," Gerd said stiffly.

"Then at least . . . let's have a little champagne."

"I don't drink at lunch," Skye said.

"How virtuous. And surprising in one no longer so young. But, fortunately, this isn't lunch. It's an assignation." Charlotte snapped her fingers, signaling for the waiter, telling him in French to send a bottle of Dom Perignon to "the handsome couple trying to hide behind the rhododendrons."

Her body, Skye noted, was still slender, her posture proud. She sat, crisp in navy linen, an expression of bemused disdain on her face, very much at ease.

"Do you want to go?" Gerd asked.

Skye shook her head.

"Good for you!" Charlotte said. "I like spirit in a woman. That's what men like too. Spirit, and a little cash."

"Stop it," Adam said. The bandaged side of his face was away from Skye. She could see in profile, in the daylight, how handsome he was, how bold his nose, squarely prominent his chin, details she had not observed the night in the square. Corn-silk yellow hair fell softly against his ear, which looked inordinately red, as though it blushed to hear Charlotte speak words deprecating herself.

"I don't mean you, sugar," she said, and reached over to touch him, cupping his square chin in her palm. "I know you love me for myself."

"Divorce him," said Adam. "Divorce him and marry me."

"What a good idea," Skye noted, buttering her bread.

Adam reached for Charlotte's hand, bent over it, kissing, his full, pouting lips making a search of her fingers. "Marry me."

"You must stop," Charlotte said.

"Yes, you must," agreed Mittri. "Didn't they teach you restraint at Harrow?"

"Eton," Adam said.

143

"Well, what did they teach you there?"

"The same thing they taught you at Cambridge," Adam said contemptuously. "It was Cambridge, wasn't it? Isn't that one of the pit stops on your road to glory? I thought Cambridge had higher standards."

"I thought Charlotte did."

"The gutter would be a step up from you," said Adam.

"Now, now," Charlotte reached for his hand, and patted it. He seized hers across the table, and kissed it again.

"I think, Dame Charlotte," Gerd said, "you have found yourself an exhibitionist."

"That's right. I'm not afraid to show how much I love her." Adam glared at him, with all the contempt he could muster and transmit through one eye. "I'm not like you, with your bloodless passion for *art.*"

"Bloodless?" Gerd reddened, his skin patchy with little spots of rage. "You anemic little—"

Skye reached under the table and pressed his knee, lowered her voice so the words would be as discreet as the touch. "Why do you even argue with him? Ignore him."

Skye sat up straighter, her posture straining for the assuredness of Charlotte's. She looked across at the older woman and wondered if Gerd could have been drawn to her by anything other than her power. He had always voiced such scorn for influence, disdain for the artists who'd been popular successes when he was not, out-and-out loathing for the less than minimal that was called minimal art, the pieces of string, little sticks of wood, letters from typewriters that had dominated galleries in the early seventies. When he'd come back from Italy and started to sell he'd laughed at his own coming into fashion, said the poverty of the "artists" who'd preceded him had created an emotional hunger for painting, made basket cases out of

144

collectors. They were looking for another Pollock, he'd said, the first one having died, like most good artists had to, before anyone would find true value, and pay for it. Cultural heroes were made, not born; publicity counted for more than brush-strokes. All of this he'd said, and then he'd married Charlotte, who could guarantee him the kind of publicity a cultural hero needed. But that couldn't have been why he left her, Skye was sure. Nothing so obvious.

She stretched her neck from the collar of the chamois mini-dress she wore, sand-colored, as her hair was now, a symphony of softness to please him. She was conscious of the advantage she had over Charlotte, the lines that were nowhere on her throat. Charlotte, too, seemed aware of that particular chal-lenge and signaled Adam to come and sit beside her, as if to show off her youth, since she could not show off her youth.

"WELL, WHAT shall we do now?" Charlotte asked after rich desserts had been eaten and coffee drunk. Adam had asked for both checks, and surprisingly Gerd had allowed him to pay. They were standing in the street outside the open wooden gate to the courtyard of the restaurant, tiny cars moving past them on the cobblestones, driving down the mountain.

"We're going to the museum," Skye said.

"How artful," Charlotte murmured.

Skye slipped her arm through Mittri's. Charlotte slipped hers through Adam's. "Shall we drive?" Charlotte asked him.

"I want to walk," Skye said.

"It's too hot to walk," Adam said.

"Not for me," Skye said.

Charlotte looked at Gerd, and back at Skye. "All right," she said. "Let's walk."

145

"I'll get the car," Adam said.

"I feel like *walking.*" Charlotte's temper cracked against the day.

"Then I'll just bring the car so we have it up there in case you don't feel like walking back down. It's a very long walk. And a hill."

"All right," she said resignedly, giving him that dominion at least over her for the other two to see. So the curious caravan made its way, half on foot, half driving very slowly, up the steep hill to the Foundation Maeght.

The sculpture museum at the crest of the hill was set partly within a beige-bricked gallery lit by sunlight filtering through blue-glassed murals by Miró, partly in flowingly designed gardens and what appeared to be an artfully arranged forest, slender pine and tall cork oak dwarfing mammoth sculptures of iron and bronze. Everywhere were statues, palpably phallic, white knobs and darts erect and thrusting in all directions, bronze vaginas cloaked with leaves of paler green bronze. Mad painted Mirós peered from totems on the patio beside mosaicked walls where a jazz quartet, plugged into an electronic system, paid riffling tribute to Charlie Parker.

"You know you never loved her," Skye said.

Gerd did not answer.

They stood on the sun-speckled terrace, where thick-footed *l'oiseau lunaire* pranced, the lunar bird of Miró, wings outstretched for flight in still more phallic thrusting, feathers and beak and eyes and crown more paeans to things Priapean. Skye tried not to think about sex, while all around her it paraded.

"Why do you stay with her?" she asked him.

"I have to."

"You have more with *her* than what we feel for each other?"

"What we feel is . . ." he shrugged. "Flesh."

146

"And what you have with Charlotte?"

He moved up the steps to a tree-shaded grove. She followed him into a tiny chapel lit by the sun purpling through stained-glass windows.

"What? Tell me."

In answer he reached for her.

"Oh, goody," Charlotte said, coming now through the gray stone doorway, Adam trailing close behind her. "A live exhibit."

Skye spoke from the circle of Gerd's arms. "We have something to tell you—"

"I think not," said Charlotte. "If anything we have something to tell you."

"Let me," said Adam.

"Not *us*," Charlotte told him. "I mean Gerd and I."

Skye looked up at Gerd's face. "Let's get out of here."

"Into the sunlight. Bravo," Charlotte cheered. "Into the truth of day, the four of us." She stumbled a little drunkenly back toward the doorway.

Adam caught her by the elbow, lost his own footing, righted himself. "Are you all right?" he asked her.

"In the pink," she said. "Or should I say, purple." She looked around the dimly lit chapel, black outlines of Jesus blessing the mauve windowpanes. "This would be too small for you, wouldn't it, darling?" she asked Gerd.

"Too small? What's she talking about?" Skye asked.

"Tell her," said Charlotte. "Why do all revelations have to be about lust? The dirty little things we do in the dark?"

"Come on," Adam said, and taking her arm moved her back toward the doorway. In the darkness, he seemed to be limping.

"How can you let her humiliate you like that?" Skye asked Gerd, when the other two had gone.

147

"I'm not humiliated."

"I am. What could she possibly do for you that would be worth it?"

"Tell her," Charlotte was saying, her face back in the doorway. And then she was gone again.

"Tell me what, Gerd?"

He walked outside into the lengthening shadows of afternoon. She followed him. He was silent. "What's so hard about the truth?" she asked him.

He went behind a hedge. Charlotte was standing there, Adam's arms around her. In front of them was a tiny pond harboring a moving metal-and-water sculpture by Pol-bury.

"Why is everyone so damn afraid of the truth?" Skye let it splash across the water. "He never loved you."

"He never loved anyone," Charlotte said. "He only loves Art."

"That isn't *true,"* Skye said.

"Yes, it is," Gerd said behind her.

She turned to face him. "What about Venice?"

"I don't remember."

"You people are truly disgusting," Adam said. "The games you play."

Charlotte turned in his arms.

He brushed away her touch, scowled at her. "You say he doesn't love? What about you?"

"I do. Yes . . . I love."

"Then divorce him and marry me—"

"I can't. It's too complicated. You don't understand estates."

"Then I'll have to leave you." He stood up to his full height, martialing his pride, wincing as his weight was distributed on both feet. "It's inevitable."

148

"Nothing is inevitable but death and taxes," Charlotte said, then added softly, "and growing old."

"What are we *doing?*" Skye said. "Adam's right. We're playing games. Why are we standing here like this? What happened to secrets? Discretion?"

"Discretion is the better part of squalor," Gerd said.

"Very good darling. When you've got enough money," Charlotte said, "you can get away with anything."

"You could be having a *life,*" Skye said to Gerd, ignoring Charlotte.

"A life . . . a life is something you pass through. Nothing will be left when I leave but my art—"

"What incredible bullshit," said Adam.

"You could have a home and children—"

"That's below the belt," Charlotte said. "Telling him what you could give him that I can't. Why don't you tell her what I mean to you?"

"Charlotte means a great deal to me," Gerd said.

"Tell her *how* great a deal."

"Stop looking at me like that," Gerd said to Skye. "Stop being so damned demanding."

"I demand *nothing.*"

"You demand everything. Watching me with those eyes, asking me to be wonderful, brilliant, pure—"

"Because you are those things."

"I'm none of them."

"Hear, hear," said Adam.

"Shut up." Gerd spoke through clenched teeth.

"He's right, dear. Gerd has the floor. And the ceiling." Charlotte laughed, a brittle little laugh, sharp, metallic, like the slim rectangles of brass and copper moving above the tiny pond. "Do you want to tell her, genius, or shall I?"

Gerd swallowed and stepped backwards, as though to place distance between himself and what he was about to say. "She's building me a chapel," he said miserably. "For the paintings. A chapel in New Mexico. The Rothko chapel in Houston. The Matisse chapel in Vence. And mine in Taos. Do you understand what that will mean? To have a monument to—"

"To you," Skye said.

"No. Not to me. To the paintings. A modern Sistine Chapel. I will do for the New Testament what Michelangelo did for the Old."

"How modest," Skye said.

"This has nothing to do with ego. This is bigger than ego."

"Not yours," she said and walked away. But she did not go far. Greater than anger was the fear he might not follow her. She leaned her face against the cool bronze of the twisted torso by Arp and waited for Gerd's long lean shadow to appear on the grass. But the sun had passed beyond the border of the trees, and she did not see him coming. His hand was sudden on the back of her neck, stroking.

"I should do a painting of you," he said softly. "You beauty."

"I have the portrait you did in college."

"You kept that?" She could hear his breath, quick, short, as if something were caught in his throat. "But I hated that picture. It didn't do you justice. You don't show it to anyone?"

"Even while you pretend to soothe me, what you worry about is your reputation!"

"No," he said. "I'm worried about yours. Someone might think you really looked like that."

She smiled at that. All she wanted just then was an excuse to forgive him. "It's all right. No one sees it. I keep it in the closet, hoping *it* will age."

"You'll never grow old." He took her face between his hands, touched her lips with his thumbs, pulling them wide, as though he would stretch her mouth into an eternal smile, fix it into serenity. "Only more fascinating. Maybe even wise. If only you could love someone who really deserves you."

"Who?"

"Yourself," he said, and kissed her.

"Ah, the tender duo," Charlotte said, appearing in the clearing.

"Why don't you take a flying—" Gerd began.

"Well, this would certainly be the perfect place for it," Charlotte said. "I'd wager that anywhere one landed, what with all the plaster cocks . . ."

"Now you understand," Gerd said to Skye. "I married her for her poetry."

"I think Adam's hurt himself," Charlotte said. "He keeps falling down."

"Any other clues?" asked Gerd.

"You know how invincible youth likes to think itself. Please come and help him."

The three of them assisted the protesting Adam to his car. He kept saying he was perfectly all right and could manage quite well alone, that he'd only turned his ankle and they should please let him go. But one time they listened and he crumpled to the ground, crying out in agony. . . .

Little by little, it seemed to me, when Skye was back recounting that day's adventures, pieces seemed to be being carved out of Adam. He was being gradually whittled away, as though innocence were a block of wood, and experience a knife.

Or maybe we had failed to note, Gerd and Skye and I included, what a blade—not so gay—was Charlotte.

SEVEN

While i waited in my voiceless vacuum for Skye to return from Saint-Paul-de-Vence, I fretted myself into a state of anxiety that only a call to New York City could assuage. The foundering of my marriage had coincided with a new phone service in the States, where for a very low rate you could dial anywhere in the country. Although there was no one I really wanted to call, in my panic I gifted myself with that service, an extravagance that at the time seemed reasonable, hysterical as I was. There is a celebrity courtesan who subscribed to a mailing that regularly listed the names and whereabouts of the world's ten most eligible men. It was her plan, often executed, to be where they were and marry them. When Jackie Kennedy married Aristotle Onassis, this woman had a breakdown, since his name had not been on the list, ruled out of consideration because of Maria Callas. The nervous breakdown expressed itself by her going to Van Cleef and Arpels and buying seven hundred thousand dollars' worth of jewelry, which she could not afford. By comparison I counted my phone service quite restrained.

New York City, despite its veneer of hard-nosed pragmatism, is riddled with whimsy, one manifestation of which is the fact that you can daily dial your horoscope. Having subscribed to the service, I began to call long-distance, on awakening, the number for my sign. Usually when you make a call, even if it's to someone you don't particularly want to talk to, there is always the chance that they won't answer, which in itself gives rise to feelings of uncertainty. So it was always reassuring to dial that number and know that at the other end was the guarantee of a greeting. "Hello, Taurus!" the recording would say, and offer cheery advice for that date. Granted life in New York is speeded up as compared to California, and they were three hours ahead of us to begin with. But it gave a certain symmetry to my day and became a harmless addiction, replacing making Elliott breakfast.

Having lost my voice (and my heart?) in the South of France, I was thrown into a state of relentless jitters, which was not helped by Sal's swinging in from the roof on a rope through one of Skye's windows, disguised as a robber, complete with hideous rubber mask. It did not bring back my voice, but came quite close to giving me a heart attack. I sat for several moments, my head between my legs, keening silently, trying to restore my breathing while he apologized. I sent him home with the written instruction not to do that anymore, and to calm myself, had the maid place a call to New York.

As they were five hours behind, and it was nearly evening where I was, the lion's share, or, as I was Taurus, the bull's share of the day's potential was already blown. But there are

154

general guidelines of truth in all things mystical, no matter how silly they appear. And like the courtesan who'd ruled out Onassis, only to have another woman nail him, I was feeling pretty crazy.

So it was quieting, even uplifting, to hear that bright little voice tell me, "Hello, Taurus!" I listened with greater intensity than I ever had, searching even the simplest instructions for hidden subtleties. "Believe only those who have your best interest at heart," she counseled me. Who were they? The doctor certainly. Doctors always had your best interests at heart, unless they were surgeons. He'd told me not to worry about my voice (why was I so worried?). Did Sal have my best interests at heart? The counsel continued to stay out of the limelight until certain details were resolved (getting my voice back?). Someone at the top (Sal, as second-story man?) was intrigued with me; I could end up having a romance with the boss' son. Now—final salvo—was an excellent time for spiritual development. I hung up the phone, feeling let down, especially at those rates.

I went over everything in my mind, making notes, examining the words like hieroglyphics for a clue to my destiny. Perhaps I had been too modest in my estimate of who was at the top. Perhaps, when coinciding with what she'd said about spiritual development, who was interested in me was God. Although it seemed a little lofty, and mayhaps a touch self-aggrandizing, you never knew, or, as it once said on a Celestial Seasonings tea box before they sold out to General Mills and stopped being interesting, "Life gives us the tests first, and the lessons afterwards." So that evening I determined to go to church, where I had not been since I was a girl, and where I'd have a better chance of attracting the attention of the boss' son.

It is key to understanding all this that I am not what anyone would consider religious, praying only on airplanes during turbulence, or when reading our weapons program. I avert my eyes when someone is injured on the street, and in the same way avert my soul from the brighter hopes, thus sparing myself in the first instance too much reality and in the second disappointment in case what we long for isn't true. I can't read without fear and pain about children who die, even though I haven't had any yet. Along with the yearning for them is terror at the thought of losing them. In a way, that's how I feel about God. That is, I *know*, but I'm afraid to hope, a confusion which believers will understand, and atheists may forgive.

Although like the doctor I was sure . . . pretty sure . . . my affliction was temporary, it was a frightening thing to be without words, especially as I was accustomed to being too quick with them, or what some might characterize as glib. Although to be in silence intensified my awareness of things I had hitherto ignored, making me more passionate, appreciative of tastes, smells, and so forth, I wanted my voice back.

I dressed in what I considered would be suitable for church, a white blouse with a bra, in case You Know Who was watching, and a skirt that was no more than demi-mini. My dressing was interrupted by the appearance of a snake that wound its way out of my closet. It was obviously papier-mâché, with a very noisy motor, so did not give me enough of a start to get my voice back, but freaked me sufficiently to put me in a rage at Sal, whom I discovered hiding behind my bathroom door.

"Did it work?" he asked. For answer, I punched him several times on his well-developed biceps. He grabbed my wrists and pressed my arms back behind me, soothing my temper and my throat with his lips. My kisses became surprisingly responsive, considering how angry I thought I was with him. Still, when

156

he eased me to the floor I resisted some, since it was my intention to be in church, and I didn't like to go with the hot juices of lust still on me. But, after all, I considered, we are in the body for a reason. So even while he entered me, and gently rocked me in my mortal shell, I worked on my spiritual development. And when it was ending, spinning us out into the Universe, damned if I didn't feel a whole lot closer to God.

THE CHURCH of Saint-Tropez, like the museum, is a stunning surprise. I had passed it several times on my way through the tiny cobblestoned streets without paying particular attention. Now that I was looking for it I saw that it would be quite easy to miss it entirely, since from the outside it was undistinguished muddy beige walls and one wooden door. There were no windows, nothing that would make it stand out from the other buildings in the diminutive village, almost as if it were camouflaged, spirit trying to pass as just another pizza parlor. But once inside, the vastness was literally overwhelming. I had been in Saint-Tropez long enough to accept a world scaled down, a certain Lilliputian sizing where all that was grand was flavor, style and the chance of love.

Within those deceptively barren walls rose a great cathedral, lit even by day with electric lights mounted in giant candelabra, and three stories above our heads a great vaulted ceiling, along the edges of which were strung like lacy ribbons stained-glass windows. Gray stone Ionic columns stretched to the roof. On the left toward the elaborate altar was a wood-carved platform, curtains lowered to half obscure it, curtains that were themselves carved from dark mahogany. To the right was a recessed hall where blazed the prayer candles. In the startling majesty, with plaster painted statues supplicating the Al-

157

mighty, little girls in white robes, hands clasped in prayer, solemnly walked the center aisle, one of them wearing a luminous hairband.

I was gratified to see that the singing was led by a woman, an energetic, handsome blonde of uncertain years who wrested devotion from the congregation with athletic immediacy, conducting the hymns like the team captain in color-war at camp. Strange as it struck me to see a European woman invested with such authority, I was reminded that half those on motorcycles in the streets of France were females, who seemed to take such honcho modes of travel for granted, as if it were their right, as long as they could afford the gas. The woman conducting the singing seemed to have the same attitude, evincing neither pride nor humility. It dawned on me that true liberation might be in doing what felt comfortable and important to you.

Beside me, Sal seemed restless and ill at ease. He had been rather startled at my request (written) that he come with me to church. Not knowing me well enough to understand that I was not, by custom, devout, he was doubtless fearful that he had encumbered himself with a religious fanatic. Either that, or he might have been himself a man of deep conviction, nervous at sharing such commitment with someone he wasn't sure he wanted for more than purposes of dalliance. Whatever the truth, he appeared quite unsettled. So I asked, in between my other silent entreaties, for God to grant him peace. Then I spelled it out so God would be sure.

When we left the church it was nearly twilight. We passed under the arch where the fishmarket was. The vendors were clearing the last of their unsold fresh catch from the ice that decked the metal tables while a man on his haunches hosed the concrete beneath. I held Sal's hand and closed my eyes and

158

took in all the smells of the port, fish, coffee, crêpes, Grand Marnier and the sea.

"Are you hungry?" Sal asked.

I nodded. As unfashionably early as it was, the day's activities, flesh and spirit, had made me ravenous. We made our way through La Ponche, the oldest arch in Saint-Tropez, and sat down at the table on the sidewalk, outside the restaurant Lou Revelen, watching the flags on the beach below billow in the dusk.

"Look," Sal said.

Thinking he was pointing to the arch of La Ponche itself, I studied the curve of the stone, red brick set in ancient gray rock. Above it was a balustrade, from which sprung cactus and oleander leaning into oncoming night, like Juliet atop her balcony waiting for her lover. A few feet below, vines had eaten through the stone, crawled through the cracks and burst full bloom above the ancient coach lamp, lit with a gas flame. In the irregular oval arch beneath, a motorcycle was parked, violating the antiquity.

Beyond acacia trees, branches wilting in the heat, was a low wall, past it the tideless, waveless gulf, solitary boats cutting across its still, silver surface. From a neighboring hotel doorway came the sound of disco music, "I Will Survive," in French, the beat, the language a challenge to despair. A woman walked by in emerald lavaliere, and a housedress. Still, I wasn't sure exactly what Sal was pointing to.

I looked at him. "There," he said, indicating the cobblestones a few feet from my chair. A new coin glittered, gold, between the cigarette butts.

I got up and bent over to pick it up, was stopped in midreach by an insolent, swinish goose. I turned, furious, and wished I could tell Sal what a lout he was, that he was behaving like an Italian street person.

"Doctor's orders," he said rather sheepishly.

I was tired of the game, fearful as he must have been by then, that nothing would do the trick, certainly none of his amateurish attempts at startling me. My lips twisted as I mouthed for him to stop it. We ate in silence, my muteness partnered by his obvious feeling of helplessness. The dish was grilled *dorade,* a local fish of meaty excellence, but neither of us showed much relish, either for food or each other. He took me back to Schuyler's house and gave me a rather spiritless kiss on my cheek, whispering "goodnight," which I took to mean good-by.

Skye had not yet returned. I went directly to bed, opening the French doors so I could smell the night, see the stars, lose myself in something bigger than my own unhappiness. I lay on the goosedown pillows, wakeful, wondering what I would do in life if my voice never returned, settling finally on writing the closed captions for the deaf on television programming.

Suddenly I felt something stir in the darkness. The curtains billowed. A shadow moved through the room. Darting it was, swift, nearly silent, but my eyes and ears were keen. My heart beat a little faster. Anger, I was sure it was, because Sal was at it again with his stupid attempts at scaring me. But in a way I supposed it was also relief, because it meant we weren't over. Then annoyance overwhelmed gratitude. I threw off the covers and slipped out of bed, moving toward the place where the shadow had been. I touched the wall. There was nothing there. I moved into the corner, felt in the darkness. No one. I went to the lamp and flicked the switch. No light came on. Had he switched off the electricity, pulled the plug? Did he imagine that, like most little girls, I was afraid of the dark?

Then I heard a barely audible rustle in the armoire. How lucky for him that I couldn't speak, the son of a bitch. Boiling, my brain reciting a litany of names I would call him if only the sound were restored, I felt my way along the wall, opened the drawer of the desk, where I had put a flashlight Skye gave me in event of emergency. I slipped the drawer shut, and quietly made my way to the armoire. Putting my hand on the key, I turned it gently and flung open the door. I threw the light on full and shone it into Sal's face. Only it wasn't Sal's face. There before me, eyes wide and black and madder than cyclones, was Charlotte, her lips drawn back, colored so dark and red it was as though she had feasted on blood.

I screamed.

"Oh, I'm so sorry," Charlotte said. "I thought this was Skye's room."

IT SEEMED that Adam had a compound fracture of his ankle. When they'd pulled up his pant leg they'd seen an exposed piece of bone. To have stumbled that badly in a sequestered place was so clumsy it gouged a great portion from my compassion, since I knew no one that physically graceless but myself. Charlotte had driven him to the Saint-Tropez hospital, where they were by now becoming quite well known, and the doctor, called away from a cocktail party, had performed emergency surgery. And this was the story Charlotte told me as she wafted out of the armoire, her explanation of why she was looking for Skye. She was sure she and Gerd, having been there for the mishap, would want to know what had happened.

She did not tell me why she had scuttled through the darkness, or what she was doing in the armoire. Nor did I ask, I was so busy shaking, finally having to go to the bed and sit on my hands to stop their trembling.

"I didn't mean to frighten you," Charlotte said, treacle in her voice, blending with the breeding, for all the world like a hostess at a garden party. "I was looking for Gerd and Skye." The voice, syrup drained from it, hardened. "Where are they?"

"I don't know." I turned the switch of the reading lamp on my headboard and was relieved to see the light go on. Then I touched my throat, cleared it, elated by the sound. Whatever nastiness she was up to, Charlotte had inadvertently been my cure. So I was polite, even cordial as I saw her to the front door and watched her float down the stairs, poor strange lady, into the night.

Immediately I went to the telephone and called Les Bergerettes to share the audibly good news with Sal. "I can talk!" I said, when he answered the telephone.

"Who is this?" His voice was heavy with sleep.

Presuming that he was being clever I laughed a gutsy womanly laugh, like the ones I had always envied, rife with experience, wisdom and sex. No more girlish laughter would come from me, now that I appreciated how precious sound was. We made plans to see each other in the morning.

I waited up for Skye to return, flushed with the day's adventures, anxious to recount them to her. She seemed genuinely concerned about Adam's injury but hardly disturbed at what I told her about Charlotte. She was so buoyed by what she was sure was happening with Gerd. She spoke with the happy certainty of a woman who knows that a man feels more than he knows. Exhausted, eyes shining, she waltzed into her bedroom before I could tell her about the reporter who had been there inquiring about Mittri, or the silence I had been jailed in. Having learned a little of the value of that quiet, I decided to keep both episodes my secret. At least until the morning when I could discuss them with Sal.

Meantime I still had a lot of energy left over. My voice was restored, along with curiosity about others, total concentration on myself having been mercifully dispersed. So I felt like making a phone call. It was still too early in New York to get the next day's horoscope. Having learned from the journalist the phrase "En P.C.V.," I decided to put it into action, since knowledge without action is only scholarship. I placed a call, en P.C.V., to the city desk of my newspaper in San Francisco. I was sure there'd be someone bright on the desk no matter what time it was, in case another civil servant was assassinated by a citizen deranged by an overdose of Twinkies. The phone was picked up by Reuben, an enterprising reporter who'd done several excellent pieces on why Dan White might have killed Mayor Moscone and Harvey Milk, besides just losing his job and a too-high level of sugar in his blood (he'd also had Pepsis), and why the jury hadn't been harder on him. Reuben's theory was that in spite of San Francisco's humanity and liberality there is still an underlying hatred of gays. One of his pieces was called "Twinkies and Milk," and had to do with the irony of homosexuals calling blue-eyed blond young hustlers "Twinkies," Twinkies being what former supervisor Dan White claimed he had eaten too many of the day of the killings, thus sugaring him up into double homicide. As an (until recently) dedicated food writer, I understand how seriously sugar robs you of your B vitamins, frazzles your nerve ends and makes you hyper. But in my eyes, a murderer is a murderer. And if Harvey Milk had been straight, and the Mayor hadn't been so sympathetic to gays, I suspect they would have hanged Dan White by his ding-dongs.

163

With my speech restored, I was filled with questions raised
by the little French reporter about the discrepancies in Mittri's
background. If anyone could turn up more information, Reuben was the one. I asked him to check with the Ford Foundation about the other two grants Gerd had been awarded, and
to please get back to me as soon as possible.

"WHAT I can't understand," I said to Sal at breakfast in the
sun-specked mist of early morning at the Gorilla Cafe, "is how
I could be so affected by a man I know is cruel."

"I don't think he's cruel," Sal said. "You were cruel to
yourself for accepting what he said as so important."

I tried not to feel contentious, knowing that he was speaking
as a psychologist, and not a human being. The human being
in him had sprung to his feet at the dinner party and literally
put up his dukes, a phrase I regret having passed from the
language, carrying as it does the implication of nobility. Men
who, being offended, put up something of their own worth,
often, one fancies, in the defense of ladies, or, to be consistent,
duchesses. "Not cruel?"

"He's a wise guy," Sal said. "We had a lot of them in the
Bronx. Guys that talk without thinking. Mittri just comes in
a fancier package."

In a way it was an observation I'd made to myself many years
before, but I hated to have someone with whom I was (once
again) infatuated let the man who had undone me, vocally, off
the hook. So I proceeded to tell him about the Inspector
Clouseau reporter person, and his revelation about the Guggenheim Fellowship. Sal absorbed the information quietly,
seeming neither surprised nor overly interested, asking the
waiter for the check as I talked. We then walked to the square,

164

which had been temporarily set up for the twice-weekly open market, which was in full provincial swing. Stalls were selling sweet-milked cheeses, fat bubbled sausages, fresh-baked pastries, dark breads with olives and raisins, apple cakes, freshly picked produce, pale green grapes close to bursting, bloated and ripe. There were ropes of garlic threaded with bay leaves and hot red peppers, tables displaying antique silver and ancient rings, cases of herb teas for migraines, insomnia, sour dispositions, happiness tea, religious objects, fabrics of Provence, blouses and jeans, lace bikini panties with feline faces strategically placed, rude joke toys: little robed friars, which when wound up sprang erections, gimmicks to gladden the cockles of hearts that loved Cheech and Chong. Beauty and piety and richness side by side with vulgarity. The same, I guess, as life.

Through it all we rambled, marking, tasting, delighting, while I myself rambled on, I who thought my rambling days were over, so to speak. I tried not to invest my diatribe with any thoughts of getting even with Gerd by exposing him as . . . what? I could not imagine why a man would have said that he had a Guggenheim when he didn't have a Guggenheim, and why, more importantly, no one had ever thought of checking out whether or not he did have a Guggenheim. Hollywood is filled with tales of men who maintained they were graduates of Yale, which lies have been exposed as parts of bigger lies. Off-Broadway has its playwrights who falsely represent themselves as having gone to Harvard. One of the flashier entertainment agencies had an employee in its mailroom who gave himself fake background, and when the agency wrote to his purported alma mater to verify the credentials, he intercepted the letter and wrote back on stationery he had had made, with an official crest, that the credentials were authentic. There are producers who buy themselves Phi Beta Kappa keys in pawn-shops, and international swindlers who change their names to the family names of heads of government, encouraging the tacit misunderstanding that they are related. But those are the high-profile arenas in which chicanery and lies are all but ground rules, and the more a man cheats, it seems, the higher he rises. Or, as a friend of mine put it, an otherwise intelligent, sensitive and well-spoken woman, "Shit floats."

But we're talking about Art here. Art in its Keatsian purity, art that made the best of the poets sing "Beauty is truth, truth beauty." Why would a man embroider, when his great gift was simplicity, when the best of his paintings, the center of his style was clarity, a technique that at one time made even the most carping of critics pronounce him "illuminated"?

But as I said, I tried not to let a glimmer of revenge glint on my peripatetic musings. To begin with, actual revenge is best left to heroes, the few that remain, now that John Wayne is gone, and it appeared to me that Sal had already claimed that role. Second, there is the principal of Karma, less Oriental and mystical than scientific, translatable into an axiom of physics: for every action, there is an equal and opposite reaction. Simply stated, that is, whatever you send out will come back at you, love, hate, anger, and so on. Or, in California terms: "What goes around, comes around." So it's best not to mess with things like revenge, lest you end up the one staked out on the anthill. Also, I have this conviction that there is ultimate justice (isn't there?), and eventually villains take care of themselves.

Not that I considered Mittri a villain simply because he undercut my concept of myself. Psychology training or no, that allegation of Sal's was valid: what had happened was my fault as much as Mittri's, not simply because of how I let it affect me but because my house was built on sand dabs.

I strode through the marketplace, trying to pick up the shards of my life, and arrange them into something of substance, while tasting cheeses and smelling all the perfumes of Arabia, which would not be enough to sweeten my concept of myself. So I pretended that I was more concerned about what would happen to Skye than to me, having watched her whip herself, once again, into the soufflé that was her relationship with Gerd, with Charlotte slamming the oven door. I desperately wanted Skye to be, as they say at est, in charge of her own life, although I do not mean to imply that est was better than Mittri, who at least never kept anyone from going to the bathroom.

Our arms laden with local goodies we had bought at the open market, we headed back to Skye's villa. She was browning, naked, by the pool. Sal was gentlemanly enough to excuse himself, saying he had to go back to his hotel for his bathing suit and would pick me up shortly to take me to the beach. The delicacy of that withdrawal surpassed anything he had thus far demonstrated, since no matter how sophisticated we may be, there is still something intimidating about a woman who has a better body.

She was oiled from high, glossy forehead to gracefully extended toe, still high from the previous day's *fredaine,* as the French call adventure (or, as I like to think of it, Bête Fredaine). She was talking, once again, about Mittri's leaving Charlotte and marrying her. The timing could not have been less auspicious, since even as we basted there I could see down the hill to where Gerd was helping Charlotte into the car, solicitous past husbandly concern. Her face was drawn; even from the distance I could see how fragile and weary she looked, probably having passed a sleepless and/or drunken night worrying about Adam. I did not tell Skye to sit up and see how far off-base she was, how bonded Charlotte and Gerd seemed to one another. My friend looked far too beautiful and peaceful to disturb. I saw no point in revving up her acids, possibly affecting her melanin, causing her to redden instead of toast.

But I did tell Sal how pathetic it all was, when he came to take me to the beach. I related to him Skye's quixotic notion of the way the love affair was going, all the while Gerd was driving off with the windmill.

"So Charlotte and Mittri are both gone?" he said, that being the key piece of information extrapolated from my tale. He turned down the driveway to the little side road. I expected him to go right, speeding us on our way to the Route des Plages and the sea. To my surprise he steered the car to the left, turned up into and around the driveway of the Mittri villa.

"Where are you going?" I asked, knowing perfectly well where he was going. What I didn't know was why.

"Do you know any of their servants' names?" he asked.

I had taken note of Skye's houseman leaning over the railing of the balcony, pining for the little maid down below, and when he pined on the phone, who he pined for was Danielle. "I'm pretty sure the maid is Danielle," I said.

Sal parked the car in the circular driveway in front of the villa, told me to sit tight, got out and rang the bell. The door opened. To my deepening astonishment he inquired of the butler in flawless French if he might speak to Danielle. In a moment a pretty young brunette in one of those lacily perky uniforms appeared. Sal extended his hand, took hers, and with the smile of a politician informed her, with exquisite diction, that she had won at LOTO, which I was later to learn is their national lottery.

The surprise on her face could have been matched only by

that on mine, since except for his ordering of wines and food, and brief disputations over price in the marketplace, I had never known Sal to demonstrate lingual ability of the word kind. It gave me to think that there were other things besides communion with the soul to be gained by silence, and foremost among those was mystery. What exactly he was about, and the manner in which he was about it were a complete puzzle to me. Danielle seemed no less baffled, claiming that she hadn't even bought a ticket for LOTO. He told her someone had bought it for her, an admirer no doubt. Her glance darted briefly up to Skye's villa, where hungered the houseman. She seemed to draw her own conclusions, accepting, as nearly anyone will, good fortune. All that remained, Sal said, was for Danielle to show some form of identification, which he would have to take to LOTO headquarters for proof, and the money would be forthcoming. She invited him inside while she went to get her identity card.

All this, I am stunned to relate, and even more stunned to realize, I understood practically verbatim, as if I had osmosed the French language through being the lover of someone I hadn't even known spoke it. A likelier explanation might have been that, having spent two weeks now in that magical country, my ear had relaxed, along with my mores, and I had tuned in to what mystics might call my Inner French. Or perhaps, as Coleridge might have put it more soaringly, it was that "willing suspension of disbelief, which constitutes poetic faith." Because what could be a more poetic form of faith than language, and what better way to understand it than to stop believing you can't. Whatever the reason, I understood almost perfectly, hearing with the ears of my love—as the next few moments I recapture with his eyes—as related to me afterwards.

The maid ushered him inside the Mittri living room, which, to Sal's surprise was rather shabbily furnished. Being from the Bronx he had difficulty understanding the mentality of the longtime rich, those in whose veins flows blood so ancient it is rusted, as is the wheel releasing their capital. The First Families seldom spend, except to endow museums and universities and occasionally the country. But of personal splendor they have little, and display less. Or as the dialogue between Fitzgerald and Hemingway might have gone, Fitz: "The rich are different from you and me." Hem: "Yes, they have less furniture." There was stuffing coming out of the sofa, tapestries unstringing and faded on the walls, fine china displayed in vitrines, but chipped ashtrays on the coffee tables. But as he was not there to spectate, he did not allow any of that to concern him, instead taking advantage of the maid's absence to make a quick tour of the rooms at the side of the house, looking for access to Mittri's studio. There seemed to be no other entrance than the big iron door on the front of the Da Vinci Bunker itself, across the patio and past the swimming pool.

He felt sure there had to be another route from the house to the studio but was unable to discover any, the doors of the den, bar and living room comprising the west wing all opening onto the terrace. The rest of the villa, in which the little maid was now foraging for her identity card, was too far away from the studio to be the logical route to it.

He did, however, find one intriguing inconsistency in the den next to the lion-carved stone fireplace. Several panels of the wall sounded hollow when pounded on, especially curious since that part of the villa settled flush against the hill and the wood appeared to be the finest, heaviest oak. He was unable to investigate further at that moment, however, due to the maid's reappearing, with her identity card. He promised her he would return it the next day, and, kissing the air above her hand, came back to the car.

"Where did you learn to speak French like that?" I asked him as he drove down the hill, Danielle giddy and waving from the doorway of the villa.

"Language was my minor," he said, which in no way satisfied me, since language was my minor, and in any of the countries where my particular tongues might obtain it would have been several months of practice and application and a love affair with a native before I could achieve his fluency.

I was growing as annoyed with myself as I was suspicious of him. Why was he so interested in Gerd, and, more than interested, sneaky? I put this to him directly, asking him what he had done in the house, at which time he answered at least that part of it, telling me about the wall. But when I asked him what he wanted with Mittri's studio, he gave me some lame answer about the French reporter nosing around and he was a little short on cash and figured he'd maybe getting a reward from the paper for information—

"I don't believe you," I said. "You may not like Gerd, but you're not the kind of man who'd do something for a chintzy informer's fee."

"How do you know?" he said, making me really steamed, because I didn't.

So we went to the beach, where I seethed in the sun for a while, wondering who this fellow really was, and whether it mattered that I didn't know vital things about him, like if he had parents. "Do you have parents?" I asked him, sitting up suddenly.

"Everyone has parents," he said. "Why don't you take your top off?"

"Where are they?"

"In Florida. With everyone else's parents. Why?"

"It occurs to me that we've been having this really steamy affair, and I don't know anything about you."

"What do you want to know?"

"Do you have brothers and sisters?"

"Yes," he said. "Why don't you take your top off?"

"You've seen my breasts. What's the big deal about exposing my breasts?"

"You just look very conspicuous on this beach with your top on."

"And it's a primary part of your training never to be conspicuous," I said. "Right?"

"What training was that?"

"Are you with the CIA?"

"I was," he said. "Now I do security for museums."

"Is that the truth?"

"I've never said a word to you that wasn't true." He looked at me with those great sable eyes and I could literally feel my heart beating in my breasts, and as I reviewed and thought, yes, it was true, this man had never lied to me about anything. More than I could say for any other man in my life. I started to undo the straps on my bikini top, because if he wanted me with brown boobs, that was what he'd get.

"Look at this." He handed me Danielle's national identity card. The card folded out in three sections. There was Danielle's picture, and all the vital statistics, not just height and weight and color of hair and eyes, but birthplace and parents and political affiliation and everything that would be on an investigator's dossier. "It really makes you appreciate being an American, doesn't it? So much more insidious than anything we have at home. There's nothing with all this information on us."

"Nothing that we know of," I said. But if I was looking to get verification of how devious our government agencies were from his answering glance, I was disappointed, because where his eyes were was on my breasts.

"You want me to put a little oil on those?" he asked me.

"I'll do it myself," I said, handing him back Danielle's card.

I lay back on my *matelas*, greasing up and feeling the curing heat of the sun, and the wetness of the oil, and the tropical glare of his eyes. "Is your father still with the CIA?"

"He's retired," he said.

I had a friend who was a reporter who believed there was no such thing as an indiscreet question, only indiscreet answers, so nothing you asked could be too much. But he had never been topless in the South of France, which is not that different from eyeless in Gaza, vulnerable as it makes you. So I figured it might be smarter to just let the whole thing unfold, revealing itself as it went along, not asking Sal any more direct questions, like did he love me, and had he grown up in his father's shadow, and was he really shadowing Mittri, and if so why? Because it was paradise enough the way it was, and I didn't want to make him lie.

WHEN I got back to Skye's villa it was about five in the afternoon. The maid told me I'd had a call from San Francisco, the caller being Reuben. There was a forty-five-minute wait to get a call through to the States, so I asked the operator to place it, "P.C.V.," and went to take a bath.

While the water was running, I walked to the window.

Beethoven was blasting in a serene way, the selection being the "Pastorale." I took it Gerd had returned and was back at work. In a wheelchair in the garden below sat Adam, or, rather, was blanketed Adam, swaddled like a character in a Somerset Maugham story in the days when tuberculars went to sanitoriums in Switzerland, languishing in the sunlight and falling in love before spitting their final piece of lung.

He had aged considerably since the evening I'd first seen him in the square with the frizzy-haired girl and the other young fellow, the three of them so carefree. It was like one of those science-fiction movies, where a perfectly decent person is invaded by an invisible alien, which begins eating him up from inside, and at some point bursts out of his chest or his throat in a manner today's filmmakers make as gross as possible to demonstrate advances in the art. Except Adam, poor thing, seemed to be being eaten up from without. There was the patch on his eye, the bandage on his cheek, and now a cast on his left leg from his toes to mid-thigh. He had the look of an old man, his shoulders slumped, his skin visibly jaundiced, his body lifeless and thin, even from that distance, even so swathed.

So now besides slashing and scarring him, she'd led him, stumbling, into his own black hole. I felt a flash of deep pity for the beautiful young man, diving into what he'd probably thought was a tub of butter, that was turning out to be a jampot filled with crocodiles.

I SOAKED for about a half hour, my newly tawny teats floating just below the surface of the water while I tried to imitate their serenity, the way they just seemed to be at peace with what was happening. Not simply going with the flow, as they say in

174

California, but bopping with the stopping, keeping with the steeping, abating with the marinating. I might have gone on like that all the way to Nirvana, maybe even enlightenment, except that the phone rang, and it was Reuben.

The Ford Foundation, although of course well acquainted with, and having only the highest words of praise for Mr. Mittri, had no record of ever having awarded him any grants. Nor did they have any official or unofficial connection with his history that they could pinpoint in their files.

At hearing this, the peace of the bathtub cracked. I asked him to contact the various other academic institutions in the U.S.A. to which Gerd's biography lay claim, including Harvard, and our own little twinkling star among the Seven Sisters, and to get back to me as soon as he had the information. Then I telephoned the Paris bureau of Time, where I had another friend, with research buttons at her fingertips. I asked her to please check out Gerd's purported attendance at Cambridge, as well as other facts of his biography, which Time always has on file in case anybody important died or in the event of a paucity of hard news, lived.

She was back to me within two days (oh, the wonder of worldwide news organizations, with their mammoth computers and diligent colonies of researchers). The news she gave me came as a shock: Gerd Mittri had, indeed, attended Cambridge University, achieving the highest honors Cambridge could award. When I say that this came as a shock, it is because by then I expected that everything about him was a lie, and it mixed me up that only some of it was. Reuben also called in, with the report that Gerd had, in fact, gone to Harvard, where he'd been graduated summa cum laude and awarded a Rhodes scholarship with which to study at Cambridge.

So that part of the puzzle at least had pieces that fit together, as did the next interlocking fragment, his teaching career at our college, all particulars of which had been verified by the Dean's office, affirming that Gerd's qualifications had been impeccable. So the middle part of his canvas, at least, was painted with true colors. It was only the section after he'd been teaching that was murky, as was the beginning of his life, because of proof of his actual identity having been destroyed to protect him from the Nazis.

We did not speak of him at all that night at dinner, Sal and I, because Skye was with us, making an obvious effort to enjoy the atmosphere of Lei Mouscardins. The restaurant at the end of the Quai Jean Jaurès had the ambiance of a lighthouse, slightly elevated as it was above the harbor, the windows on one side looking across to Sainte-Maxime, the other facing the Mediterranean. The two rooms were candlelit and warm, the food of an excellence starred by Michelin. But there was a sadness to the evening, in spite of the succulence of the *poussin*, a tiny chicken stuffed with its own innards and grapes.

I was ill at ease because I knew something that Skye didn't know, and that was that in *some* part of his life, Gerd Mittri was a phony. Skye was downcast because her great question—why had he left her?—had been answered: a chapel in New Mexico. It wasn't good enough. Sal was ill at ease because he knew more than either of us, and didn't want to tell what or why.

It was in nearly every way a joyless evening. I don't think any of the three of us was aware of where we were, or how delicious was what we were tasting, how fresh the air we were breathing, lightly salted and easy on the nose, gently brushed as it was with the wetness of the sea. We weren't conscious of how fortunate we were to be where we were, and attractive and healthy, unlike Adam, who sat a few tables away from us. A

176

scotch plaid shawl was around his shoulders, like that Maugham-ian invalid. His crutches leaned against the window, behind his chair. He seemed in a kind of drugged half-dream, his hand so unsteady as he lifted his spoon that most of the soup spilled back into his bowl. Finally, he abandoned even trying. The frizzy-haired girl had to feed him, while their other young friend looked on with baffled concern.

Adam did not raise his eyes, as though the dish he had eaten most of was his own mortification. A mosquito hovered near his face, charging his cheeks; he did not pull away. The girl put down the spoon, half rose from her chair, and with two hands, slapped the air next to his nose, killing the insect. She looked over and saw me watching her, and smiled with regret and embarrassment. *"Bon soir,"* she said very softly, as if she knew I understood how painful it was to see a vital young man made so feeble.

"Bon soir," I said, more softly even than she, because there was something sticking in my craw. I had never been sure exactly what a craw was before, but now I'd found it.

Somehow, for all of it, I blamed Mittri. What his uncaring-ness had almost managed to do to Skye, inside, Charlotte seemed to be doing to Adam's exterior. As one makes little patterns on the tablecloth with the tines of a fork in a moment of stress, trying not to eat too much bread, I tried to design in my mind what might be the function of these people's lives. It could not be solely to destroy.

I had seen the passion, the conviction with which Mittri taught art, the thoroughness with which he communicated his gifts. He himself had not come into conspicuous flower as a painter until he was well into his thirties, after his sojourn in Rome. While most people assumed it was the contact with so many dedicated teachers and artists that had pressure-cooked his potential, I suspected it was the spiritual strength he drew from Skye. It was as though she had taken a tithe on her own divine essence and offered it up to him, consecrating a piece of her soul, feeding his creative psyche with her own spark.

She would have disclaimed all this, of course, so modest and self-effacing she was in her own estimate of what she could offer anyone that she had probably blocked out how empty his early work had been. Only once had she admitted that she had been in any way sustaining to him, and that the night she got drunk and spilled her chalice of longing and regret on the table.

So it was a strange night that the three of us spent at Lei Mouscardins, with that other trio a line of tables away, two of them trying to restore their broken friend. I called to mind how young and uncomplicated they'd appeared that first night in the square, how beautiful Adam had been. Now, he hunched like escargot with the meat extracted, a crooked shell.

It blazed through my brain that maybe the joke I'd made once to Skye had been right on track. Maybe the reason there was such an obfuscation of facts about Gerd's birth was that his true place of origin was Transylvania, and instead of seeking access to his studio, Sal should have been looking for the crypt. Somehow it all had such a strong, Draculean whiff to it, with Adam there, being gradually drained of his bodily fluids, and Skye next to us, a part of her vital essence sapped.

Maybe who Gerd and Charlotte really were were Mr. and Mrs. Dracula. And they never drank wine. Just a little champagne.

EIGHT

A FEW DAYS LATER Adam had the bandage removed from his cheek and the patch taken from his eye. There is, in history, a moment to which disaster can be traced, an actual trigger, as with the assassination of the Archduke Ferdinand at Sarajevo, and World War I. In personal history as well there is doubtless an instant when life comes to a crisis point and the subsequent course of that life, whether it is to be one of exultation or tragedy, rather than the mixed bag most of us get, is determined. With Adam, I would pinpoint that time as the afternoon he saw what had been made of him.

I remember when I was a little girl and would read fairy tales the two phrases that hung most hollow in the air around my eyes were "Woe is me!" and "What's to become of me?" I think even at that age I had a distrust of self-pity, as often as

I was tempted to feel it, sensing that to roll around in feeling sorry for yourself was literally to flounder, to rob yourself of the energy vital to continue and change. In the same way "What's to become of me?" was an affront to my innate respect for self-starting. Somehow I knew that the world batters the passive, as a dog will always sniff out the one who smells of fear. So when those weepy heroines whimpered, "What's to become of me?" I responded in my mind with the eight-year-old equivalent of Who gives a fuck?

Still, there are some in this life who are palpably acted upon, and one of those was Adam. I realize that destiny is arguably self-determined, that it was he who had placed himself in Charlotte's hands, surrendering what might have been a jollier memoir. Probably he had a weakness in his spirit, a wish to be coddled; I'm not sure. I never actually got a chance to talk to him, and I doubt he would have shared his philosophy with me, assuming he had one. But as one reconstructs the events of that day, it is possible to imagine with what horror and loathing he viewed what had become of him. And to murmur, with heart full of pity, "Woe is he."

The slash to his cheek had severed a nerve, paralyzing the right half of his face, leaving him no control over the muscle, so that the flesh drooped down to his lip. Trying to smile, he could move only the left half of his mouth. The right side was slack, lifeless. All he could manage was a grotesque grin.

His right eye had also been affected. A splinter of glass had cut the cornea, and in healing, a white mucousy film had formed, an actual cloud on the surface of the eye. So although he had some vision, the eye itself was sinister, as though there were in him some dreadful phantom, an apparition forming, struggling to release itself from inside him even as one looked

180

at him. And tried not to look away.

He could not close the eye. The doctor advised him he would have to tape it shut or wear a permanent patch to avoid chronic irritation from not being able to close it. And all this time, Charlotte sat weeping, moaning, into a handkerchief. It was she, finally, who had to be sedated.

According to Charlotte's chauffeur they drove from the hospital to Charlotte's yacht, where Adam awkwardly made his way on crutches up the gangway. The two of them sat at anchor, under the canopy on the deck, and drank more than just a little champagne, becoming very rowdy and vulgar, cursing, hugging and reviling each other by turns. The sedation the doctor had given Charlotte combined with the wine to send her raging out of control.

From the deck of the yacht berthed next to theirs, the producer's mother angrily advised them she was holding a seance. If they didn't keep the racket down, she threatened she would call the harbor police to deal with them or, more fittingly, the beasts and banshees and demons of hell itself, who were standing by. At that moment Adam stepped to the rail and gazed at her wordlessly, and she ran screaming back into her cabin.

Charlotte had her steward make sandwiches and pack them into a picnic basket along with a gun. It was her plan, presumably, for the two of them to go off in the Captain's tender, have a last meal, let Adam shoot her, or shoot herself, or shoot a hole in the boat so the two of them could drown together. But she was too drunk to make it down the ladder to the boat, and the descent was impossible for Adam with the cast on his leg. So instead they got even drunker, and passed out on the deck in each other's arms, Adam with his eye glaring open.

OF ALL this, at the time it was happening, we were unaware. Skye had gone into town to pull together an enchanted little dinner for herself and Gerd, *à deux*. Sal had brought fresh croissants and brioches still warm from the *boulangerie* to the villa. We lavished them with lavender honey we had bought at the open market, *miel* as sweet as the melons of the province, the color and texture of cantaloupe meat, but smooth-skinned, miniature and more tasty. Every once in a while he would step to the edge of the sunlit terrace where we breakfasted to check the activity down below. It was not long after Charlotte and Adam drove off in the limousine on their way to the doctor that he literally sprang into action, seized my hand, pulled me out of the house and into his car and the two of us zipped down, around and up into the Mittri driveway.

"You stay here," he said. "Honk the horn if they come back." He went to the door, rang the bell, and when the butler answered, asked for Danielle. While the butler went to get her, Sal slipped a piece of tape on the front door lock. It was crisply and efficiently done, with the secure expertise with which he made love, albeit with none of the time-taking or flourishes.

In a moment Danielle appeared, flushed and excited to see him, gratefully accepting the return of her identity card. He informed her that full proof of her identity had been accepted, and the check was being drawn. Now all that remained was for her to send a telegram to LOTO headquarters in Paris, acknowledging that she was free to accept her prize, that she had never been convicted of a crime and that she owed no money in taxes. He gave her the address where to send it, and suggested, with some urgency, that it be done as quickly as possible to expedite payment. To ensure that everything be accepted as official, he advised that the butler go along with her to the post office to witness the sending of the telegram, since things had

182

to be done in an official manner. She said she understood completely, which of course she did not, and went to get the butler.

They were both back forthwith, the butler protesting what he considered the lack of logic of his having to go along, insisting he would be perfectly willing to say he had witnessed everything even though he hadn't. Danielle looked at him askance, her eyes moving discreetly to Sal's, to make sure he noticed her uprightness, and repeated, like a little song, that these things had to be done in an official manner. Smiling to show how brightly she imitated Sal's tune, she got into the car beside the butler, and giving her benefactor a thousand thanks, waved good-by.

We preceded them down the driveway, turning to the right, as though continuing on to someplace else. Sal stopped the car at the side of the road and watched them disappearing in the rearview mirror.

When the other car was out of sight, Sal turned his car around and doubled back to the Mittri villa. "Honk if anyone comes," he said, getting out of the car. And then, expertly, he slipped the lock and was in the house.

I got out of the car. From the studio seeped choral music by Satie, the singing of angels who had discovered a new century, and with it, harmonies that permitted optimism and despair in almost the same breath. It was suddenly replaced by Stravinsky's *Symphony of Psalms.* I could only imagine Gerd had decided that whatever he was painting would benefit from a little rebelliousness and discord, devotional though its intent might be. The music began to inspire a little rebelliousness in me too as I wondered why I was stationed outside like a stage-coach driver riding point when there were no Indians. Charlotte and Adam were off on an obviously lengthy excursion.

There was no way the maid could get back to the post office, send her telegram and be back in less than half an hour.

So I followed Sal into the house, leaving the door slightly ajar, as he had done, in case we had to make a quick escape. From what? I wondered, my heart beating in a way I was not accustomed to having it beat, since I don't go to fright movies anymore, now that the gore oozes from the screen and pieces of the actors fall into your popcorn. When I was a little girl I used to watch horror movies through a buttonhole in my coat, letting it close when the events on the screen became too much for me. *Psycho* I watched for the first time with my head in my second mother's lap, returning six more times in an attempt to build courage, seven being the mystical number for every great search, a cabalistic doctrine I was intuitively aware of, even though I did not know what cabalistic meant at the time. Like some refugee from *Gulliver's Travels,* I was speeded by instinct toward any mastery I could get. By the sixth viewing, I had witnessed through my buttonhole—the coat dragged with me into spring, and summer—everything but the shower scene. The seventh time was the occasion of my first date, with the son of a man my mother was seeing, who, my mother attracting those of like parental bent and affection, was home *very* briefly from military school. He suffered from asthma, which seemed particularly out of place inside a uniform. His epaulets appeared loose and trying to tear themselves away from him, as if despising his weakness. He kept touching my breasts, which were not even developed, in some pathetic militaristic assault his classmates had probably advised would make a man of him, divesting him of his wheeze, the only option he had besides moving to Tucson. People kept turning around to see the perpetrator of the terrible noise, as though there were a fouler fiend in the theater than Anthony Perkins.

And there I sat, his hand on my not-quite breast. I felt so degraded I forgot to hide my eyes, and so saw it all, the stabbing, Janet Leigh's nipples, everything. It was several years before I was able to take a shower, many months before I could take a bath without a friend, parent or housemother present (even an unkind one) and then, never with the plastic curtain closed, so seared into my eyeballs forever were the shadows behind it.

Understandably the children of today are a puzzle to me, delighting as they do in being terrified, the more hatchets splitting the skull, the bigger the box office grosses. The Phantom that once prowled the Rue Morgue has fathered a legion of apes skulking the movie industry, the filmmakers themselves, rewarded in direct proportion to their lack of taste. But with it all I have faith in children and can't understand why they accept, even relish, such mayhem. I have two theories, the first being that the young are inherently more moral than their society thinks them, and the license with which they have been endowed sits less than serenely on their psyches. In these films mutilation and murder always follow the victim's sexual encounter, as if there were literal hell to pay for humping. Like Republicans in long-ago France, spectators applaud the thwuck of the guillotine, considering such punishment well deserved. Either that, or the world has become such a frightening place, with such devastating weapons, such grim potential for us all to be incinerated, that an axe murder in the woods is like a trip to grandmother's house.

Well, so there I stood, my heart beating as fast as if the lights were out, not knowing what to expect, hoping Sal would not be angry with me for deserting my post. He was in the den, his hands on the carved stone mane of the lion's head above the fireplace.

185

"I think I've found it," he murmured, excitement at his discovery apparently overpowering any annoyance he might have felt. He pulled the top of the lion's mane toward himself. There was a groaning sound; a panel of the wall sprang open. A boom of choral voices, ushering from the dark passageway before us, thundered around our ears. "Lau-da-te- Do-mi-num," drummed the words, praising God to music that seemed to be calling up darker deities.

"Stay here," said Sal, and started into the shadows.

I obeyed him for what must have been two seconds, moved in equal part by curiosity and a sudden, punishing fear of the light. The den in which I stood alone seemed as fraught with menace as did the flickering screens of my youth. I hurried after him, darkness appearing infinitely more safe, since it contained Sal, my surrogate buttonhole.

We were not to stay in darkness for long. At the other end of a short tunnel, carved into the hill, was Gerd's studio, ablaze with light and music. In the midst of it stood Gerd, like a great conductor, hovering over both music and the art. On one curve of the wall was an ink sketch of a body on a table, near it a figure of miniature radiance. There were two easels, each of them supporting half of a vast canvas on which was being painted, in the druggy, adolescent style of figurative expressionism, a magnification of that small sketch, which I saw now was Christ with Lazarus, on a life-support system. In front of the easels, on high wooden stools, paintbrushes in hand, sat the young girl with the frizzy hair, and the young blond boy who'd been Adam's other companion.

Gerd had his back to us. "Poeticize the sky," he instructed the boy loudly, his words arcing over the irregular tempo of the music.

The boy glanced up and saw us standing there, and seemed

almost to smile. Gerd followed the direction of his eyes, turned, and saw us. I have never seen a man crumble before, his posture literally collapse, as though he, himself, were a house of cards and life, finally, has revealed itself as nothing more than wind.

"Take a break," he said to the two of them, and shut off the music.

He waited until they were gone, vanished through the passageway back into the house. "Those are my apprentices," he said, trying to keep the turmoil out of his voice. "I let them do some of the basic work on the easier parts."

Sal just stared at him. I think I kept my eyes more on the floor than Gerd, because I don't like to see anyone debased, not even one for whom I have no real personal sympathy. In fact, in his humiliation I understood more about him than I ever had, his bitterness at his acceptance, the irony with which he spoke of painters who sold, the dedication with which he taught us at school, overlaid with a kind of sorrow when relating anecdotes of his mentor Hans Hofmann, who had, in many opinions, been a better teacher than painter.

So even though Gerd had dug the pit himself, I didn't like to see him on the edge of it, ready to fall in. Cloaked as he had always seemed in arrogance, I cringed for him, at standing there so naked.

"It's not unusual," Gerd went on, the words beginning to come in a rush, "in a work of such magnitude for there to be helpers with areas that do not require inspiration and then the painter himself the creator comes in and makes it his own—"

"Keep it up," Sal said. "I've heard of your brilliance as a lecturer."

"The master-apprentice relationship has been fundamental to art since the Middle Ages," Gerd said, sweating now, his breath squeezed in a torrent of words. "To be steadfast guarantees stability, fine workmanship, deep satisfaction on the human level with the master acting as guide. So when the pupil goes off on his own he is ready for life . . . And of course it's convenient for the master, having his colors prepared, his canvases stretched. It's good to have someone who can do the dull bits. Art isn't something you do by yourself, like poetry or philosophy. It has been like this since Giotto learned his craft in Tuscany. So much is lost now by painters who think they don't have to be pupils. Van Gogh was a pupil of his cousin Anton Mauve. Matisse of Gustave Moreau. You must nurture students and bring them to fruition. Loyalty gives strength—"

"That's funny," Sal said.

Gerd's eyes narrowed. His posture straightened slightly, the prospect of combat giving him back some of his spine. High above him, the round skylight dispensed an eerie brightness, ricocheting sunlight through the cold, circular, concrete room. Everything looked sterile, bleached out, colorless. Gerd's face seemed robbed of blood, no pigmentation in it, only his eyes gleaming topaz, a trapped cat's eyes. "What do you know what is funny. What do you know what is serious, security man. Do you have any idea what this is?" He gestured at the canvas.

"A lie," Sal said.

"You with your little mind, your little ambitions. How could you even begin to imagine?" He smiled now, touched the edge of the painting with his finger. "It is the job of art to reflect its time. Christ in a modern context. The new Sistine Chapel. Birth, death, resurrection. And this"—he pointed to Lazarus —"will be at the center of the dome. Construction has already been started in New Mexico. They will come from everywhere, it will be a shrine—"

"To a painter who couldn't paint," said Sal.

188

"To art," Gerd said. "To God, to the God who shows himself through art."

"But not *you*. Not yours."

"Why is it important if it's mine? Why isn't it enough that it just *is?*"

"Is it enough for you?"

"It would have been," Gerd said, and started pacing, his long-legged stride inhibited by the dimensions of the room, the clutter of paints in cans, brushes soaking, piles of stereo equipment, boxes of tapes and records, completed portions of canvas piled against the wall, like disorderly memory in an overtaxed mind. "But you know how America is. It doesn't honor ideas, it honors success. It forgives everything as long as you're a success. So don't assault me with your integrity, child of the CIA. Integrity counts for shit in your country . . ."

Sal turned to go. He reached for my hand, drawing me toward the open place in the wall.

"What are you going to do?" Gerd asked.

"You figure it out," Sal said.

"You owe me a fight. There is a challenge in the air between us."

"Okay." Sal turned and looked at him. "Your choice of weapons."

"Good." Gerd smiled. "Still holding to a sense of fair play. The noble American."

"Just let me know when?"

Gerd nodded. "Until then, maybe I could prevail on you not to say anything about . . ." He indicated the clutter around him, the rubble of his life revealed . . . "this. Maybe we can find some, you know, gentlemanly solution."

"An odd word coming from you," Sal said, and we left.

So THERE it was, as plain as the nose on someone else's face. Just about the premier painter of his day, master of all he surveyed, but not really. It had probably been like that ever since the beginning of his actual success, only his early painting the creation of his own hands. Which explained almost all of it, his brilliance as a teacher, the flatness of his early work, the life that had seemed to spring into it in the middle seventies. Maybe his curse had been being as smart as he was, knowing too much, intellect chaining intuition, the true gift of the artist. In Rome probably he had found his first "apprentices," the hungry young people with the gift, who were willing to exchange it for money, like the classical guitarist in the square in Saint-Tropez, who'd given his song for a bowl of soup. Like Matisse himself, who'd traded a canvas for a meal at La Colombe d'Or.

But where had Gerd gotten the money? If the Guggenheim and the Ford Foundation hadn't funded him, who had greased his very fast track? It hadn't been Skye. She'd told me often how he'd refused to take anything from her once they were back from Rome except a meal or two hundred. Who'd provided the loft where he'd gone, ostensibly to paint, before he was "discovered" by the critics and his works began to sell? Who'd given him the means to continue, the pieces of silver to bribe others to further the cause of art, and betray themselves?

It was a curious conundrum, but one about which I could not ask Sal. His jaw was set in that grim, determined line I'd come to recognize as signaling the end of a discussion. We made our way out of there. He told me to go ahead and wait for him in the car. But as was my new custom I disobeyed, and hung back a little. Peering through the glass of the entryway, I watched him put an electronic device on a lamp.

THE VARIOUS terrible scenes between Gerd and Charlotte which took place over the next couple of days were later reconstructed, partly from the testimony of their servants, partly from speculation on the part of the police, and for me, partly from the listening equipment I found in Sal's luggage. Having never been on the front lines of journalism, and being less interested in a good story than a man who, if not pressed, might really love me, I did not question him relentlessly, since it was obvious he had said as much as he wanted to about why he was in France. I was, however, an indefatigable sneak, and listened in on the earphones while he was in the shower. Fortunately, he liked himself squeaky clean, so I got to eavesdrop on what I suppose was most of it. I sat riveted on the floor of Sal's closet, an earphone in one ear, the other cocked toward the bathroom so I would hear when the water stopped running. What I heard through the listening device seemed electrifying at the time, although, in view of what happened, it turned out to be sad. Tragic, really, if we don't have to have the stature of kings for our falls to be ill-starred, calamitous. Now cracks a noble mind, I kept hearing, as if I were in the back of a Shakespeare seminar questioning whether there is any less pathos in the splintering of a not so noble mind.

"I've killed him," Charlotte was saying, as I listened through the electronic equipment. I could hear her pacing the cold marble of her living room floor, heels clattering on the hard slippery surface, staccato, like her breath was. It was evening then, just after seven. She was back from the yacht, still drunk, or drunk again. Her words were slurred, tongue thick with wine. Contempt hung heavy and cold from the edges of her speech, icicles of self-loathing. "I've killed Adam."

"Then why is he still walking around?" Gerd asked her. "Or

is that his ghost in the garden? What have we here, Hamlet's father?"

"How fabulous to be you," Charlotte said. "With your wit, and talent. Your magnificent talent."

"Stop it," he said very softly. "I don't need your sarcasm. Not tonight."

"Sarcasm?" Charlotte said. "You think I'm not sincere? I, your greatest supporter, your strongest advocate. Builder of your goddamned cathedral in the desert?"

"I know what you've done for me." His voice was as heavy with shame as hers was with wine.

"Why, I've protected you in private, defended you in public. Taken your side no matter who dared to attack you. Even . . ." Her voice broke. ". . . even that poor boy out there. That boy who loved me as you could never love me. As you could never love anyone."

"I don't think you should drink any more."

"I'll do whatever I want. I'm allowed to mourn him. He's dead, and I've killed him. Did you see his face?" Her heels clicked on the floor as she walked to the window. "Look at him. He's a monster. That beautiful boy." Her glass fell to the floor and shattered.

"Leave it alone. I'll pick it up. You might cut yourself."

"What concern. What kind concern. Why couldn't I have done that the other night? Why didn't I drop the glass before I could touch him with it? Why didn't it fall out of my hands?"

"You can drive yourself crazy, tormenting yourself like that."

"I am crazy," she said, so coldly I could feel a knell of recognition in the pit of my stomach. That's right, I thought to myself. That's been there all along. When you're rich enough, they call you madcap, a padding of respect between

192

you and the world, when what it should be is a wall. Now she's said it herself. Everybody run away, while you still can.

"I want you out of here," she continued after a moment. "Take your society whore and go away. There's gas in the little Mercedes. It's my farewell gift to you. That, and half a million if you leave me now, this very minute. So I can be with what's left of him."

"You can be with him," Gerd said. "I don't care. I don't have to go."

"Yes you *do*, you *do*, you *do*," she said, the vowels spinning now, like circles in the eyes of cartoon coyotes when they've been hit on the head. "He'll only stay if he can marry me," she said. "You heard him say it."

"But that was before—"

"Before?" she said. "Before what? Before the bandages came off and he saw that I'd maimed him? You think a little thing like that could sour such a sweet nature?"

"Charlotte—"

"Don't *touch* me, don't you dare try to comfort me. Comfort me by leaving. Go, take the car, and the money. Miss Duncan has enough for both of you, but I know how *proud* you are. How it bothers you to take money from a woman. Unless it's enough to subdivide a desert and build a cathedral." She stumbled over a piece of furniture, and gave a little cry. "Don't help me," she said angrily.

"I want to help you."

"Then leave. Leave now. The keys are on the hall table. Get out of here."

There was the sound of a door opening. For a moment I thought that Gerd had decided to take her offer, or had walked out of there in rage, or humiliation. But then I heard Adam's voice. Plaintive, it was, broken, like the boy himself.

193

"Charlotte . . ."

"My darling." Pity edged the affection of the greeting.

"I have to talk to you."

"Leave us," she said sharply.

"This is still my home," Gerd said.

"Find someplace else. I hear she's very clever with decorating, your slut. It will give her a challenge. Find someplace and let her fix it up."

"I'll be in the bedroom," Gerd said, his footsteps echoing on the cold terrazzoed floors.

"Don't you want to sit down, darling?"

"I've gotten awfully good with the crutches," Adam said. "See?" He made a speedy circuit of the hall, rubber tips squeaking.

"Please . . . you'll hurt yourself."

"What's left to hurt?"

"Oh, darling . . ."

"Don't *look* at me," he said.

"But I love you . . ."

"Then you really musn't look at me."

"I've told Gerd to leave," she said, taking a deep breath, filling her plans with the forced enthusiasm of a cruise director announcing future events. "I'm divorcing him. We'll be married, just the way you wanted."

"Just the way I wanted." Irony clung to the phrase like barnacles.

"We'll stay here. Or live anywhere you like. Palm Beach, Deauville, Tangiers . . ."

"I think Tangiers. More freaks there."

"Adam . . ."

"I wouldn't want to feel too much out of place."

"You must stop."

"No. *You* must stop. Stop pretending you still want me."

"But I do. Oh, Adam, please. Don't make it harder than it is. You must know how I despise myself."

"But I don't despise you," he said. "I love you. Too much to saddle you with a horror show."

"Don't say that. You're my beauty." Her voice broke.

He moved to her on his crutches, let them fall against a chair, put his arms around her. "Beauty dies," he said, and wept along with her.

THERE IS a lyrical village called Ramatuelle, its look as lovely as its name, winding up a series of hills about twelve kilometers south of Saint-Tropez. As Saint-Tropez has an interdiction against any new building, which preserves its charming antiquity, the diminutive size of the town, constructed, like the arches of its fort, to accommodate a race of shorter men from centuries before, so does Ramatuelle guard its medievalism. The town winds inside a massive stone wall built by the Saracens in the fourteenth century to protect the city from invaders as it now protects it from modernity. For all that every third doorway on the cliffside, climbing, is a tiny *bistrot*, mostly featuring the kinds of pizzas found in Nice, thick-crusted with cheeses more redolent than the bland, chewy mozzarella advocated by Italians, the town itself still has the flavor of ancient Gallic times. In summer there is nearly always in progress a festival of town Arts and Crafts, set in the center of the blocked-off road, lace, wood carvings, painted porcelain, smooth, sanded rocks, split to display jewellike centers, polished fine. Cornering the Arts and Crafts display is a souvenir shop with apple-cheeked dolls in antique attire, sitting at spinning wheels, or guarding their flocks, and, once again, the herbs of Provence, wrapped in the fabric of the province, bright little cotton sachets, red and green and yellow and bright blue, printed as with an ancient seal, a few francs less than in Saint-Tropez.

I gave myself fully to the joy of beating the one shop in Saint-Tropez whose proprietor I found unpleasant by buying several sachets of the spices she sold for more money. And with the many francs I now imagined I was richer by, I bought one of the dolls, a shepherdess, the word for which in French, I had learned, was *bergerette,* the same name as Sal's hotel. (The Lord is my *Bergerette,* I couldn't help thinking.)

Dropping our booty in the back of Sal's car, we went to have dinner, down a steep hill we maneuvered on foot, leading out of the town. The place we chose was a traditional restaurant, Auberge de la Favouille, which that night served the specialty of the region, Chicken Bonne Femme, with boiled potatoes. The potato is halved and inset with sprigs of pine needles before being roasted, so the pine, along with fresh rosemary, infiltrates the taste of the potato as the heavy pine scent at night assails the nose. The pine for the potatoes is pulled from trees directly adjoining the restaurants, trees that terrace the adjacent steep hill, descending almost perpendicularly from the walled mountain road encircling the town.

We sat on the candlelit, lantern-globed terrace, pretending life was simple. There were a few lights in the farmhouses below us in the valley and deep ahead of us in the lengthening shadows of night. At our backs the hills echoed crimson, vanished rays of sun still clinging to their shoulders. Wisps of clouds streaked radiant purple past the horizon. The lights in front of us in the distance gave the illusion of fireflies, so small were the bright inroads they made in the oncoming gloom. Occasionally flamed actual fireflies, lending a brief incandescence to the warm green darkness. I felt a part of a more pristine past, an air of antiquity accompanying dinner because of the gentleness of candleglow illuminating the tables and the few lights down below.

But suddenly there was a great, unexpected blaze of light. So fast that I was hardly aware of it, not even clearly conscious of what was happening, I heard something bouncing down the curve of the mountain above us, crash through the ancient stone wall. Sal was on his feet, the look on his face of someone who knew exactly what to do, but knew at this moment he could do nothing except push me out of the way. The car hit just below the terrace where we dined, turning over several times before exploding and bursting into flames. All around me was screaming; I realized that some of the screams were mine. As soon as anyone could get near the car, and the fire had burned itself out, it was discovered that there was more than one body inside, in what was left of a small Mercedes.

THE IDENTITY of those who perished that night was deduced the next day when the disappearance was reported to the magistrate of the young man and young woman who had been studying painting with Gerd Mittri. Also found in the wreckage was a burned but complete plaster cast, in a better state of preservation than the leg it encased.

Apparently they had been so anxious to get away that they'd taken the keys from the hall table and driven off in Gerd's car. A note was found in Adam's room, expressing his regret and grief to Charlotte, advising her that he had no choice but to run away. In spite of her protests that she loved him still, he wrote, he knew she was just being kind, wonderful woman that she was. The others, fearful of their future because of what had been exposed, had decided to go with him. They would send her money for the car as soon as they found jobs and could afford to repay her.

I am sorry to report that the contents of the letter were repeated almost word for word in Paris Match and, as the canvas of misfortune widened, were translated worldwide into all papers owned by the purveyors of gossip and sensation. Someone in the Mittri villa had, apparently, seen Adam's note, more or less memorized its contents and sold it to the scandal papers. Probably that bitch Danielle, impatient at not yet having received her check from the Lottery.

The most remarkable underside of the accident was that even with the amount of damage, the automobile having been gutted by fire, such was the quality of the workmanship that the authorities were able to discover the brakes had been tampered with. Poems are made by fools from Hades, but only Deutschland makes Mercedes.

NINE

THERE IS a tide in the affairs of women, a little lapping of fate against their shorelines, to which they hardly pay attention, so busy are they waiting for their ships to come in. The moon, of course, controls those tides, that same inconstant moon Juliet didn't want to swear by, the very moon that measured Titania's menstrual flow and caused me to cancel my subscription to Ms. In England there is a whole breed of nannies who believe that the full moon, when coupled with an east wind, causes diapers to go green. More babies are born when there is a full moon, and more people die. Superstition aside, people are more likely to get into fights and eat donuts. The full moon has likewise been credited for werewolves, vampires, and, of course, lunatics, from whose ancient name their very madness is drawn.

But it is love, I think, that drives most women crazy. Either the longing for it, or the frustration of its promise unfulfilled, or the getting of it, and losing it, or the never finding it, or the feeling that it is undeserved, or the fear that he doesn't appreciate enough to bestow it, or the nagging suspicion women feel, even when they are brighter, that men know something they don't know, and that is why love is less important to them. As if it were weakness instead of strength. So the fault, dear Brutus, is not in our stars, or in our moons, but in our love that we are underlings.

And it was love, I understand now, with awful clarity, that made Charlotte go completely mad. I don't like to speculate on the little chips of privilege that fall on such a woman in her childhood, the fine china bowls in which porridge is served by the governess, the tiny carousels that spin in the tuliped gardens outside, the rooms with the private tutors. But I'm sure she was spoiled, pampered, stuffed into noisy crinoline petticoats, paraded in front of relatives who didn't hug her enough. I have a vision of her as Little Lady Fauntleroy gazing out the windows of her ancestral estate, as some of us board trains late at night with the hope in our subconscious luggage that he'll be on this trip, only to look out and see that elusive pair of eyes in the window of the train traveling in the opposite direction. Where was the fairy prince at the bottom of Charlotte's garden? Who was the one who would rescue her from the loneliness?

Her marital history, after the several seasons of debutante parties where she was the one who glowed most visibly, garnering the roses (one of them Billy, who regretted shortly before his death that he had never married her, or dated Rhonda Fleming), was well known. After the movie actor, and the shipping magnate, and the racing driver, and the general, I guess she looked to Gerd the same way Skye did, as some sort of cultural hero who would endow her with sensitivity and grace as she would endow him with the means to immortality. That he was not only not her man but not even his own must have struck her as extremely vulgar, since the thing these people understand better than anyone is good form.

The fear common to all women with a sexual nature is that they will never find their great love. Each of us is born, I think, with an innate hunger, which I will call the R-spot, intersecting somewhere between heart and hotbox and head. From infancy we reach out, and are cuddled enough to make us used to affection, or not cuddled enough, and so become hungry for it. As soon as we can hear and comprehend, even parents who neglect us tell us fairy tales, featuring the prince who acts as a palliative for the main disease of women: having no kingdom of her own. If the Kingdom of Heaven is within, as Gerd's centerfold tried to tell us, then why is the Kingdom of Heaven for women always without? Why was the cure, or at least the healing balm that didn't exactly get rid of the disease, but at least covered the symptoms, a man? I think it goes past conditioning, goes past nature, goes past history, maybe even goes past Jesus, as tuned in as he was, or he might have also said the Queendom of Heaven is within. I think what it goes back to is the Creator Himself, who really likes a good story. And if it wasn't for women yearning, questing, their little R-spot palpitating for Romance, please, just one Romance to fill up my R, all we'd have would be war stories, mysteries, and spy thrillers. Not that there isn't room for those, too, but I imagine every once in a while, even God could do with a lift to the spirit.

But back to Charlotte. In spite of all the publicity, the adoration in the press, the papal princes who regularly pledged her their fealty and estates, her great love having all her life eluded her, how comforted she must have been by the presence of that boy. How he indulged her, filling her glass more than it needed to be filled, perhaps, but at least being there to pour, on call with caressing and caring. When she heard it was Adam who died in the car crash that night, she ran quite literally mad. We could see her careening around the garden below us, tearing up flowers, screaming, taking great clumps of grass and throwing them into the pool, wads of dirt from the roots muddying up the water while the echoes of her protesting denials ripped through the countryside. "No," she shrieked over and over again. "No it isn't possible. No! *That* isn't who it was!" And then she ran into the house, calling for him, crying out his name, "Adam! Adam!" Like a mother calling her little boy, who was being naughty and playing games with her.

"You can come out now," she sang, almost merrily. "I won't be angry with you for hiding. Come out now," she called, the play disappearing from her voice. "Come out," she cried, frantic. "*Adam,*" she screamed. "A-A-D-aam." It was a shriek of mortal agony, a woman being buried alive.

She stumbled back, dead-eyed, into the garden. Gerd stayed with her, at careful distance, trying to get her inside. But she threatened him with the garden shears, aiming them at him, telling him she would cut off his head.

The doctor arrived and tried to calm her, but she filled the air with obscenities. It took three people to hold her while the doctor gave her an injection—Gerd, an obviously terrified Danielle and the butler. At last she was quiet, and they carried her inside. But every once in a while would come, like the tolling of a great bell, a moan so sorrowful and wild as to strike pity into the heart of Attila the Hun, or a Hollywood producer.

EVERY TIME they make another discovery at Pompeii I find myself feeling annoyed at newspaper accounts of the scientists' latest conclusions. Each corpse unearthed, in a posture to indicate he fell, sword by his side, without any warning, suffering searing, instantaneous suffocation, the rushing lava giving him time neither to escape nor breathe, nor maybe even mercifully consider his own end, gives new fodder for their postulations, and in some way affronts me. First, because there is such hand-clapping at the state of preservation, the bones being in a condition to yield disclosure of what people ate, their physical activity, occupations, the diseases that afflicted them. So it begins to seem, as in a war movie made for purposes of propaganda, that they died so others may live, or, in this case, learn. Second, someone interviewed at the excavation site inevitably speaks of scenes of tragedy and pathos. Words to me are as sacred as art was to Gerd, though I try whenever possible to use my own, and tragedy and pathos have special meanings. Tragedy, I was led to believe, as a student of Shakespeare, only pertained to those with a noble nature who suffered from a fatal flaw, in Macbeth's case ambition, in Othello's jealousy, and so on. Pathos, by the same token, is inspired by events, speech, or art that gives rise to emotions in the spectator, sorrowful or tender feelings, which I find it hard to work up over an old corpse with a sword.

The more skeletons they find, the more gleeful they are, like Rumplestiltskin dancing around convinced no one will ever guess his name, their conviction being the latest allotment of spines will enable them to discover truths about that society. But they are anthropologists with shovels, and those of us who deal, however faultily, with words to try and unearth secrets do better to excavate the living. The more people who die without expressing the hope and longing and happiness and sorrow they feel, the less likely we are to understand what life really is, or what it could be.

Everybody dies. How they die makes a difference. How we die can be fascinating. But how we live is what really matters, how we deal with pleasures and hardships, challenges or boredom. Our words are the index to our lives, not the way our bones lie. Which is why I get in a solemn snit at the smugness of those diggers, imagining for a moment that they can determine what those people were, and so elicit emotions for them.

Hard for me then, impossible, really, to accept the unexpected closing of that ancient Mediterranean resort as riddled with "pathos." But pathos was something I felt a terrible sense of, watching Charlotte in the garden below, totally unhinged by the death of that boy. For Adam I felt unqualified pity, mostly because he'd been so beautiful. No one said women were always deep, or even discerning.

It was Charlotte, of course, who had sabotaged the Mercedes. Charlotte who meant the brakes to fail, but surely not for Adam. Trying to provoke Gerd into leaving her, urging him to flee with Skye and the money, she had already tampered with the machinery. Like most heiresses, she tried to squeeze something out of every relationship, as with the trusts she was used to and could trade on, of the money kind, the only sort of trust she had. Her knowledge of cars was what she had milked from her third husband, the racing driver, who'd taught her enough to make her safe on the highway, or someone else unsafe, before himself being killed at Le Mans.

It was not so much that she hated Gerd as that she loved Adam. She knew he had meant what he'd said about leaving, unless they could be married. In a kind of beleaguered self-hypnosis, she imagined she could salvage of his honorable intentions what could not be salvaged of his face. She had wanted to marry him as quickly as possible, and murder, as anyone with lawyers knows, is less time-consuming and costly than the courts.

All this was to be learned later, after the skein of sorrow and madness unraveled even more. Some of it I gleaned for myself, listening in on Sal's headphones to the conversations taking place in Charlotte's villa. But I did not share my discoveries even with Sal, reluctant to let him know I was spying on his spying. I waited till he was in the shower to eavesdrop, grateful for his cleanliness, which seemed nearly as obsessive as my wanting to know.

"I killed him," I heard Charlotte saying. Her speech sounded doltish and thick—not the thickness of booze but of sedation.

"You musn't talk like that," Gerd said softly.

"But it's true. I did it. I killed him. First I killed his face, and then I killed him."

"It was an accident."

"No. I fixed the car." She sounded almost giddy. "Of course I didn't mean it to be him. I meant it to be you."

He did not answer her. The silence was as weighted as her words had been.

"You'll want to leave me now."

"You have another car you want me to go in?"

"I don't blame you for being cruel. You must go to the police, tell them what I did. You'll do that, won't you?"

"No."

"But I must be punished."

"You'll punish yourself."

"You'd like that better, I suppose." She gave a deep sigh, as though air could cure as thoroughly as oblivion. "Where is that silly boy, Adam?" she suddenly asked.

Gerd did not answer.

"Do you think I should write to his mother?"

"Why?"

"Basic good manners," Charlotte said. "To ask her permission to marry him. Do you think she'll give it? They're peculiar people, the English. I don't think she'll mind my being so much older, as much as how many times I've been married. Will you talk to her? You have such powers of persuasion."

"Of course," he said after a moment.

"You can be so kind when you want to."

"You'd better rest now."

"Are you leaving me?"

"No."

"But you will, I'm sure you will. You couldn't possibly forgive me for trying to kill you."

"Yes, I can," he said softly.

"But how will I ever forgive you . . ." she said, ice closing over her words as the lava rushed over ancient Pompeii freezing forever the revelers in postures of pleasure and flight . . . "for not being the one to die."

I MUST note that during this baffling time a strange diffidence seemed to have settled over Skye, as if the presence of all this madness and tragedy next door, the deaths of three young people and Charlotte's raging out of control had too much reality for her. She seemed strangely quiet, stunned, I presumed she was. But she was also a little aloof, as though she didn't care to acknowledge what was going on. Like shoppers in an inflation who worry about the price of food until their country is at war, and they understand what real troubles are,

206

she might have seen how relatively carefree her longing for Gerd was when measured against death that came too soon and a mind that cracked. And rather than diminish her own agony by seeing how proportionately pain free it was, she chose not to focus on the blitz that was occurring down below.

Not to say that she was less than a caring human being. No one had more courage outside love than Skye, no one was less likely to turn her head and pretend that she didn't see when it came to the big issues. Certainly not anybody in her financial bracket who wasn't running for public office or whose husband wasn't. But this was happening, quite literally, too close to home. She'd been so filled with belief that everything would work out that the untoward events of the past days were too overwhelming, holding as they did in their shadowy corners the dark promise that nothing might work out at all. She took note, or at least seemed to, of each grisly revelation as it unfolded. But in her eyes was a certain lack of attentiveness.

I can forgive that in her as she would forgive it in me. We all long to be central in a saga, and do, in fact, star in our own soap operas until we are preempted by bulletins, the shooting of Sadat, the attempted assassination of Reagan—all of which take our minds temporarily off the problems we consider so riveting. The prospect of nuclear holocaust makes the fact that our mother didn't love us, or our lover might not, pale. Which is why, I suppose, people don't think about it very often, except those committedly concerned who think about nothing else.

I cannot be one of them; it is like thinking always of death. Not that the prospect of oblivion doesn't make me crazy, not that I don't want to scream when I hear the proponents of nuclear buildup in our own administration say that with enough shovels we can recover from a thermonuclear war— that is, all we have to do is dig ourselves under three feet of earth and wait for the rays to go by. Ha. Couldn't Jerome Kern make a song out of that one. But that is lunacy of such high order that it couldn't even excite pathos in an anthropologist, since there will be no bones or swords lying around to determine what we ate for breakfast, or what diseases we were suffering from, since there will be only one, and that one madness.

But, as I said, we all like to focus on our personal dramas, and Skye was no better than the rest of us in that regard, seeing her romance as totally galvanizing, which is not easy to maintain when people next door are being killed and going nuts.

I did not try to add to any measure of Skye's pain, or numbness, autoanesthesia being a gift I hadn't realized she had, by telling her what Sal and I had discovered in Gerd's studio. I was ashamed for Mittri, as if we had caught him masturbating or picking his nose, something John Barth could have made central to a man's downfall, but I found disgusting. I had likewise prevailed upon Sal not to share that revelation with her. He told me not to worry, that wasn't his job. At that point I again tried to find out exactly what his job was, but he reiterated that he ran security systems for museums and galleries.

Pressing, since I didn't believe him, I asked him what galleries and museums, for example. "The Whitney," he told me. "Sotheby Parke Bernet."

We were at the quietest beach in Saint-Tropez, a curve of pebbled sand on the gulf, in front of a restaurant called Les Catamarans, which is very low on chic but has the best *moules* in the area, big fat ones they are, almost suicidal in their deliciousness. (Even in the midst of tragedy, or pathos, life does go on.) There was a dock stretching out a little way into the

208

still water, from which a motorboat occasionally took off with water-skiers, and we sat on it, Sal meditating on the paddleboats with their duos of vacationers pedaling around the harbor, and the windsurfers, expert on this side of the hill, brave and valiant in a very soft wind.

"What do you do for Sotheby Parke Bernet?" I asked him, folding my *Herald Tribune* across my knees. In spite of all that had happened and was happening around me I was raised in the East of America, where newspapers were newspapers. The South of France had restored in me a passion for clarity, so I woke every morning with a rapacious appetite for that day's edition of the *Tribune*, which I looked forward to as I would a meeting with a lover. Naturally I concealed the depth of my heat for the paper from Sal, as I would any other infidelity, knowing how greedy I was to be feasting in so many areas. The Emma Bovary of Glut.

"I monitor their alarms systems, provide them with security guards," he said, matter-of-factly. "Investigate any claims of falsity or forgery."

"Had any lately?" I asked him.

He shrugged. "There are always discontented collectors. People who get bidder's remorse."

"Bidder's remorse?"

"Think they've paid too much for a work of art in the heat of an auction."

"And could any of those bidders who felt such remorse have bought a work of Mittri's?"

"There were inquiries." He looked across to the rounded mountains that were Sainte-Maxime, his dark eyes set in kind of a hurt squint, as if his brother had just accused him of flirting with his wife. At least that's how it looked to me, but then I

209

did not have that much experience of hot-blooded Italians who were also in the investigation game. Maybe the sun was just in his eyes.

"What kind of inquiries?"

"Anonymous letters," he said, and shrugged. "Suggesting that some of the Mittri canvases auctioned there might not have been authentic."

"Sotheby Parke Bernet, and France *Soir*," I said. "The author of these anonymous letters is obviously a person of ecumenical tastes."

"Either that, or he had a good address book."

"He?"

Sal narrowed his eyes even more, as though the accusation of lust had extended to his niece. "I think it was Adam. Who had a better reason to try and expose Mittri as a fraud?"

"Why not Charlotte?"

"She had nothing to gain. She already knew about him. She might have wanted him dead, but it was pointless to have him dishonored."

So he had obviously listened to the tapes, probably when I was in the shower. And he knew now that Adam's death was Charlotte's fault. How did it work on these international levels? Wasn't it his job to go to the local police, because his only visible, public assignment on these shores was to wire the little museum by the harbor?

But I did not ask him that, for fear of seeming impertinent. He knew what his job was. I still had the feeling he was not telling me everything, especially whether or not he loved me. But my friend who was never afraid to ask indiscreet questions was dead. Not as a direct result of anything he's asked, I don't think, but no longer an example of how to act, having had his action curtailed.

Besides, foremost in my preemptive editing of questions was the sweetest prize in our relationship: that Sal had always told me the truth. I didn't care to force him into a position where he'd have to lie.

I was weak now from the heat of the sun, and trying to sort it all out like the jumbled words in the *Tribune,* and the feelings I got from watching the darkly handsome, grim set of Sal's jaw as he studied the harbor. His arms were around his naked knees; he sat slightly hunched in his trunks, as though himself trying to click things into place. By now I was sweating from the relentlessness of the rays, the stillness of the dock in the motionless water, the confusion in my head. And I still hadn't figured out what word could be made out of RODIF. The print from the paper was coming off on my thighs, abetted by the sweat dripping from my naked breasts, which, things having come to such a seemingly comfortable pass between us, Sal didn't look at out of the sides of his eyes anymore.

"Are you hungry?" he asked me.

"For food, you mean?"

"For food." He smiled. I nodded. He helped me to my feet, hugged me once to his naked chest before I wound the scarf around myself.

He kissed me. "Fiord!" I said, the electricity of his touch jangling my brain.

"What?"

"The jumbled word," I explained. It was then that I experienced what a devout Catholic might call an Epiphany, a moment of sudden, blazing clarity, where one sees through to the heart of Faith, and finds in its burning center the truth, and that is, *it's all okay!* I suddenly understood it all, as the word had unwound from RODIF. Whatever happens is okay. If it doesn't go the way you wanted it to, the way it goes will work out more interestingly. If someone doesn't love you, it's okay. If they do, it's even better. The thing is not to force it.

But, of course, knowing something, and putting it into action are two different things, even for the spiritually illuminated. I followed Sal to a table set in the sand. He pulled out a canvas chair and I sat, sinking a little. Then he moved an umbrella to shadow us, so my shoulders wouldn't burn. He signaled for the waiter, a slender young man in very tight jeans, and ordered some wine.

"Do you care about me?" I asked, my own death wish as strong as a plump mussel's, though not as unselfish.

Sal looked past me to the water, where a white-haired windsurfer, probably in his sixties but flat-bellied with well-muscled legs, skimmed the water like a teenager. His sail was red-and-yellow-striped, the brief bikini he wore the same brilliant blue as the sky. "I'd like to learn to do that," he said.

"Care about me?" I said.

The waiter brought the wine, the Château Minuty Rosé Cru Classé we had come to drink as a habit with our meals. There might have been better wines, just as there were many roads to heaven. But some things felt perfect as they were, like orgasm. The waiter poured a little in Sal's glass. He sipped, looked up and nodded his approval. Both glasses were filled.

"To not being afraid to say you care," I said, lifting my glass in a toast.

"I think," said Sal, "I liked you better when you couldn't talk."

He took me back to the villa after lunch. I had been squelched by his comment, just as I had by my housemother's all those years before, not because I had no right to wonder, but be-

212

cause, except for the period of my enforced silence, I didn't know how to keep still. I admired people who did, like the beautiful girl on the beach, her scarf waving in the wind, her feet hardly seeming to move as she wafted along the sand, her presence a proclamation of tranquility. Peace, of course, is harder to find in this life than even love. Those of us who find the second so elusive get into a panic about priorities so often we never even struggle for the highest joy we can attain, and that is no struggle at all. This is something I understand with special pain at funerals, when they say "He is at peace," and I think, wrong: he just isn't here anymore. Peace is something we would do better to achieve while we are alive, when it would do other people some good. Because an occasional volcano aside, the natural state of the world is really Eden, and what the serpent brought wasn't sex, but restlessness, our inability to leave well enough alone.

And that includes me, with my big mouth. I stood by the window of the living room in Skye's house, wondering if I would ever see Sal again, or if I hadn't really made my own bed this time. My self-absorption was temporarily scattered by a fascinating scene taking place in the landscape down below. Charlotte was apparently feeling better. Like a slightly dotty Mary, Mary Quite Contrary she was out in the garden seeing how it was growing, after having ripped it nearly to smithereens the day before. She was wearing her nightgown, like an invalid of the spirit, joy drained from her face, dutifully watering what was left of the flower beds around Gerd's studio, sprinkling them with an oversized metal watering can.

The bell rang. I hoped it was Sal, embodying forgiveness and patience, virtues I would try to incorporate into my character, if only he would come back. From down below came the deafening crashes of clashing chords from the *Symphony of*

Psalms, a strange echo of the scene we'd been witness to the day before, with Gerd so shamefully exposed. I wondered what he would be doing in the studio, now that his hands were cut off, now that those poor young people who'd painted for him were gone. How long did it take to recruit the truly gifted? Did Sal intend to expose him? And what was the point of Gerd's even being down there, trying to paint?

As became clear the moment I opened the door, none. Gerd stood in front of me. "May I speak to Schuyler?" he said. His very manner was an apology, his carriage so broken he could not even be described as a shadow of his former self. To see shadows, there has to be light. He looked destitute, stripped not only of his reality but his pretense.

"Come in," I said. I found myself reaching for his arm. He seemed suddenly fragile, like an aunt whose company you've never particularly enjoyed, and usually avoided. Then all at once you realize she will not be with you many more afternoons, and wish you'd been kinder.

"Thank you," he said, humbly, as for a penny in a blind beggar's cup. I went to look for Skye, stricken, and shocked, at how grateful he was. She was sitting at her dressing table brushing her hair, as she'd been doing the night of her dinner party after he'd insulted her, not a care on her face, Ophelia drifting downstream.

"Gerd is here," I said.

"Good." She brightened and went to her closet, reaching for some smart designer number, as though where it was all leading now was a Diana Ross concert.

I followed her into the living room. Gerd was sitting, hunched, on the piano bench. He did not look up or turn as she touched him, but reached for her hand, pulled it over his shoulder, and, moving it next to his face, kissed her fingertips.

"Did they tell you?"

"About Adam and the other two? It's horrible. Just horrible." She leaned and cradled his head against her breast, kissing his hair.

"I mean, did they tell you?"

"What?"

He turned. "About the invasion of my studio? What they found?"

"No."

He looked at me, a puzzled expression on his face. Then he told Skye what Sal and I had discovered, reviling himself, as Charlotte had done, for not being the one to die the night before.

"Stop it," Skye said. "Don't talk like that."

"Do you hear what I'm saying?" He was on his feet now, angry, because he finally saw himself clearly, and she could not see him. "Doesn't it mean anything to you that my whole life is a lie?"

"Why did you go to so much trouble?" she asked him. "Why couldn't you just be the great teacher you were?"

"Do you have any idea what it is to *know,* but not be able to *do?* To have in your head what you can't put on canvas? To understand fire . . . and not have the flame?" His big, long-fingered hands struck the piano. The sound was harsh, discordant. "To love with a passion, and not be able to express that love?"

"I understand that," Skye said softly.

"Do you?" He turned and looked at her. "So much fuss over love between man and woman. I'm talking about love between man and art, man and God. Because art is all we have in us that's holy. Not to be able to touch the God in yourself, to feel it's there and not be able to connect with it, do you know what that does to a—?"

"You didn't have to pretend you were something you weren't," she said.

"But that's what they want," he said. "The pose." He saw how she looked at him, and waved her glance away, as though it was more than he could stand. "Stop looking at me as though you still loved me."

"But I do."

"How can you? I'm not what you thought I was."

"Of course you are," she said, and went to the hall closet. She opened the door and took out the portrait he'd done of her all those years before. "I've known all along."

I won't say the portrait was totally devoid of talent, but it was empty of inspiration, empty of Skye. Not so much far away from what she looked like, as were the women in Picasso's paintings, but with neither spark of its own nor glimmer of her. Cold, professional, constipated, filled with technique and no art.

"I know how you painted," Skye said. "I knew your work. I could tell the new work wasn't yours."

"Then how could you love me?"

"Because I love *you*. Not what you do."

Thinking back on that scene, I realize how riveting it must have been. Otherwise I might have noticed the smoke; otherwise we all might have noticed the smoke. Because by then it was pouring into the room, great, black belching clouds of it. When we ran to the window we saw the studio below, consumed in flames.

So it hadn't been water that Charlotte was sprinkling, but gasoline. And through it all, like the confused screaming of a devil who'd found God, came the *Symphony of Psalms,* praising, praising, praising.

OBVIOUSLY SHE'D thought Gerd was in the studio. He related to the police what she'd said to him that last afternoon. They agreed that she'd been in a murderous frame of mind. The doctor's testimony substantiated the fact that she was unhinged. Danielle had seen her slipping the iron bolt on the door outside the studio but had paid no particular mind. It was not unusual for there to be much secrecy about who went in, and why. And there was always insistence that strangers be kept away, and no one should see the paintings.

Danielle had been working in the kitchen when she'd smelled the smoke. With the quick thinking she'd come to expect of herself since winning at LOTO, she called the fire department. Because of the terrible forest fires the summer before, the firemen were in a state of great preparedness, both the full-time *pompiers,* and the volunteers, fifty of them in all. There were five huge Berliet fire trucks with oversized black rubber tires, and Renault cars and jeeps manufactured for precisely such an emergency. Considering Saint-Tropez was a resort, with a leisurely pace attending all its activities, including, one would assume, averting disasters, the speed of the fire trucks' arrival, the heroism and dispatch with which the firemen handled the blaze, was nothing short of staggering. In addition to using hydrants, they'd siphoned water from the pool, fighting the flames so well that even the brush on the hillside was spared. Nothing was lost except the studio itself, with all of Mittri's paintings. The true tragedy of the affair, everyone noted.

At least, that seemed to be the tragedy. Not until they

217

started clearing the debris did they find Charlotte. As reconstructed afterward, she had ignited the gasoline, and not thoroughly satisfied that Gerd was in the studio, had gone to make sure, entering through the den to the secret tunnel. The spring on the paneling, from all indications, had slipped, closing her in, her screams drowned by the choral music of Stravinsky. When they found her, she was kneeling at the base of the panel, hands clawing at the wood, dead of smoke inhalation.

She wasn't even burned. That was the wonder, the firemen having smothered the blaze before it could even blast through the tunnel or reach the main structure of the villa. It made everyone feel more secure about their personal safety that summer, with life in the hands of the *pompiers,* who'd come a long way since Pompeii.

TEN

So it was gone, rubble, the dream, the delusion, the lie, even the trappings of the fantasy, those piled up canvases against the wall, waiting for their chapel. They say it's the job of art to heal rather than rupture, a good witchcraft to the spirit, where the self of the painter reaches out to the viewer and touches something in him that makes him more whole. But with Gerd it seemed the job of his art, community effort though it may have been, to reach out to the painter and make him conscious of what he was: in this case, ashes.

There was a great family dispute about where Charlotte was to be buried, angry telegrams from lawyers, phone calls from nieces and nephews concerned with their place in the will, sharp instructions from bankers and trustees, who wanted her remains returned to the family plot in Southampton. But Gerd insisted on her being buried in the garden of the villa. It was, he said, the place where she'd been happiest, not adding that it hadn't been with him.

The service was tiny and sad, Charlotte laid to rest where all the blossoms had been before she'd ripped them up, with Gerd instructing the gardeners to cover her with flowers and plant them where she lay. A few members of the international set, having read of her death in *Nice-Matin,* and having no more exciting plans for lunch that day, motored in from Cannes, and seemed annoyed that it wasn't a grander gathering.

I felt sorry, because, horror, madness and attempted murder aside, she was a woman from one of the first families, and not one living relative was there to drop a tear or a daisy on her grave. It seems the bluer the blood is, the thinner it flows.

Gerd looked truly pitiful, stricken as a man can be only when he knows a woman has tried to kill him, and doesn't blame her. His flame had gone over a cliff, and now, with Charlotte, the fantasy itself had died, the castles in Spain, villas in the South of France, and citadels in New Mexico. From his mournful appearance, it was hard to believe she had ever said an unkind word to him, much less tried to murder him twice.

Afterward we went back to Skye's, where she'd laid a mourner's repast, ripe with reminders that life had to go on, and while not being a bowl of cherries, was at least celery remoulade. Nobody ate very much, except for the group in from Cannes, who after realizing that there were no hot dishes to follow, opted for a proper lunch at Le Club 55. Sal sat beside me, thoughtfully crunching an apple. I could hear his teeth breaking through the skin. He had been at my side constantly since the last, terrible event, silent and protective, in a kind of patient attendance that I knew went past our relationship, and had to do with thoughtfulness and a sense of obligation, not wanting to add to the turmoil until the rest was finished.

Soon the minister left, followed by the few people from the village who'd been there, and the prefect of police. And it was just the four of us. I could see Skye studying Gerd, not wanting to move too quickly, before the body was even cold, in this case, too cruelly accurate a metaphor. Every once in a while she'd put her arm around him, soothingly, and he would sit there, not responding.

It looked to me like he felt as dead as Charlotte, with everything over as it was, including the deception.

"What do you intend to do?" he asked Sal finally.

"We'll talk about that in private."

"Ah, good." The life came back a little into Gerd's eyes, the start of a smile pulled at the corner of his full lips. "The duel. I'd almost forgotten."

He was wearing the garb of the mourner, a dark suit, with a plain black tie, as if he'd come to the South of France with the perfect wardrobe to feel good in, and a slight proviso for death. Skye reached for his jacket, helped him off with it, hanging it up in the hall closet, closing the door quickly so he wouldn't see his portrait of her languishing inside, and be reminded of how talented he wasn't. She went back to the couch where he sat, loosened his tie, opened the top button of his shirt and rubbed his throat. He stopped the motion of her hand.

"Can I talk to you alone?" she asked him.

"That won't be necessary," he said. "We are among friends here."

Friends? I looked at Sal. But he was too busy exchanging glares with Mittri to notice. There probably is no more powerful scrutiny in the world than a man and woman on the verge of falling in love, except two men about to do battle.

221

"You don't mind if I speak in front of them?" Skye looked strangely beautiful in black, like Joan of Arc, sexed, with long hair. There was a useless valor in that choice of role, since three of us in the room knew what she could not accept—that she had no future with this man, that her voices had deceived her.

"I have no secrets from these people," Gerd said with restrained irony.

"Good," I said. "Then I have a question." He looked at me, his eyes as lifeless as the young hands now were that had painted for him. "Where did the money come from?"

"The money?"

"There were no Guggenheims or Ford Foundation grants. Where did the money come from?"

". . . Portraits," he said. "I painted rich women. They sent for me. Fat Europeans who wanted my company, and settled for paintings."

"Then why all the secrecy? Why the mystery? Why the lie about grants?"

"I was building a history," Gerd said. "It's boring, most of the time, the truth. Nothing that will enliven an obituary."

"You can't live for your death," Skye said.

"I am afraid," Gerd looked off, "it may prove the most interesting thing about me."

"Listen." She touched his chin, lifting his face so he had to look at her. "You have nothing keeping you here anymore. Let's go home."

"Home? To what?"

"To be together."

"But there will be no more paintings. I have no future. And everyone will know I don't even have a true past. At least they will . . ." He looked at me, and then at Sal, something in his eyes past pleading. ". . . if your friends . . ."

222

"I don't care if everyone knows," Skye said stubbornly.

"Women," he murmured. "No wonder you have so much trouble sleeping, when all you believe in is love."

"What better thing to believe in?" Skye asked, or rather stated.

"Oh, stop being such a wimp," I snapped at her, and looked at Gerd. "What do you want us to believe in? Art, the way you do?"

"Good point," said Gerd.

"Don't grade me." I turned on him. "This is not one of your seminars."

He turned to Sal. "We'd better go somewhere and finish it, before she takes me on in your place."

"What's your choice of weapons?" Sal asked. He wasn't smiling. It was frightening.

"Words," said Gerd. "Words at twenty paces." He grinned. "The brave man does it with a sword, the coward with a pen. I would suggest paintbrushes, but, as you already know . . ." He shrugged. "I'm not very good."

"Okay," Sal said, heading for the door, still dead serious. "Let's do it."

"How dumb," I said. "All this combativeness. So much easier than being a real man."

"And what"—Gerd looked at me—"is your definition of a real man?"

"A real man is someone who isn't afraid of a real woman."

At that moment, Skye applauded. Flushed with her own momentary realization of what she was, what we both were, maybe what we all are if given enough credit, especially by ourselves, she stood up, very straight and very tall, and planted herself squarely in front of him. "Don't go," she said, not a whimpered request but an order.

"Stay here with me. I've always believed in you. Whatever you wanted to be, you were. I've worked my whole life to be good enough for you."

He looked at her, his dark yellow eyes remorseless. "I never wanted a woman who was good enough for me," he said, and stepped around her.

I must say, at that moment, watching Sal walk behind him down the steps to the driveway, I felt a twinge of regret that all it was going to be was a battle of words. Because somebody should have killed him.

As THE chauffeur was later to testify at the inquest, he drove Gerd and Sal in the limousine to the yacht, anchored by the third quay. It was not the most companionable location Charlotte had chosen, being as it was the farthest away from the comings and goings of the transients, who, even when kings and movie stars, had had for her the glamor of travelers on Greyhounds. The ship was almost totally isolated except for the smaller yacht anchored aft, where the movie producer's mother entertained a gathering of gypsies, who danced a tarantella on the deck.

The accordion music, and violins, on which they all but played "Zigeuner," somewhat obscured Gerd's words to the chauffeur, dismissing him for the evening. He also told the steward he was free and could go into town, where the captain of the vessel was already roistering.

After a little, the gypsy music stopped. There was a glittering peace on the harbor, the sea having cooled to cadmium green beneath a violet sky. The waning moon brushed the darkening evening with shy luminosity.

Gerd invited Sal into the saloon, where he poured them both

a drink. "So now you can tell me," he said. "What really brought you to Saint-Tropez?"

"Sotheby's got wind of possible fraud involving your paintings. They sent me here to investigate."

"What do you intend to do?"

"My job."

Gerd sipped his drink. "What's really to be served by your telling them? Obviously I won't be trying to paint in the future, much less hoping to sell anything. Why take away the value of what's already done? What's to be gained?"

"Truth. Some justice."

"You're a little webbed around the eyes to be a Boy Scout," Gerd said. "It's grown-up time. What do you want?"

"I don't want anything."

"What a lucky man you are. No ropes pulling at you. No desires. No twinges of corruption. Still, even Abraham Lincoln might have enjoyed a villa in Saint-Tropez. It's yours, Sal. You can have it, you and Mimi Sheraton."

"No, thank you."

"Then let's approach this philosophically. The paintings exist. They are no less art because I didn't do them. Why cloud their worth?"

"I think you should save your gifts of persuasion for women."

"Women don't need persuasion," Gerd said. "They persuade themselves—"

"Let's get on with it," Sal said. "How do we do this . . . duel of words?"

"We do it like this. I say hello . . ." Gerd pointed a gun. "And you say good-by."

He motioned Sal toward the companionway.

Sal preceded him to the deck below. At the bottom of the

stairs hung a double set of chains. Sal grabbed them, pulling them taut, letting them spring backward toward Gerd, knocking the gun out of his hand. It skittered along the floor. Gerd started after it, but Sal's elbow caught him across the chest and drove him back through the doorway into the corridor.

Bouncing back off the wall, Gerd lunged at Sal. Sal brought his knee up hard between Gerd's legs. Gerd fell, sprawling, holding himself, coming to a thudding rest on the floor against the wooden paneling, his head lolling on his chest. Sal moved to him. "Are you okay?" There was no response. Sal bent over him. Gerd's head butted him under his chin, sending him flying.

"First you kick a man in the balls, then you ask if he's all right," Gerd said, moving toward the gun. "No wonder Betty Crocker is so crazy about you."

Sal saw the fuse box on the wall, opened it and flipped the switch, plunging them into almost darkness. One blue-shaded light from a hurricane lamp still shone dimly, reflecting back from the glass box on the corridor wall, where a fireaxe was mounted. Sal shut the door to the stateroom. The corridor was eclipsed into total dark. There was a shot, a muzzle flash in the blackness, the sound of a bullet ricocheting.

Sal shinnied toward the place where the fireaxe was, took off his shoe and, feeling in the dark, broke the glass. He grabbed at the axe. Another shot rang out, another flash from the muzzle rent the darkness.

Down on all fours, crawling, the two men listened for the sound of each other. Sal could hear a door open. He followed the noises, the squeak of a drawer opening. Moving toward the sound, he got to his feet in front of the doorway, raised the axe and flung the door wide open.

Gerd heard the crack of hinge against frame and fired in

226

Sal's direction. At that moment, Sal hurled the axe. It thudded dully into something. He held his breath.

A flashlight went on, catching in its beam the dangling axe, fixed in the wooden paneling of the wall. "Nasty," said Gerd, flashlight in his hand.

Sal made a lunge for the axe. Gerd moved forward and pressed the muzzle of the gun to Sal's ear. Uncertainty played briefly on Gerd's lips. With a quick movement of his wrist, he struck Sal with the gun, knocking him unconscious.

THE DETAILS of the confrontation were wrested by me, blow-by-blow, from the survivor, who, I am delighted to say, was Sal. Occasionally, life gives us justice; at least life does when it isn't imitating art.

I would guess that Gerd's unforeseen sense of decency came as much of a surprise to him as it did to Sal, and the rest of us, when the facts of the encounter became known. Only Skye seemed to breathe a sigh of "of course" when she found out Gerd could have killed Sal but did not. I did not dispute her contention that that was how Gerd was in all things, secretly wonderful, because by then, Gerd was past argument.

To reconstruct the rest of that night, according to a yachts-man coming back to harbor about ten o'clock, he passed a captain's tender heading out to sea. There was a man at the wheel, singing at the top of his lungs, zipping along in front of the wake he was making in the water, ripping along the tear he made in the silence. It was a strange song he sang, according to the yachtsman, who considered himself somewhat of a lin-guist, a tongue he did not recall having heard before, odd, filled with "Ums," and "Dominums."

Later that night, farther out to sea, a fisherman heard a loud report, which sounded to him like a shot. Two days later they found the captain's tender from the Mittri yacht floating a few miles out to sea. In it was a gun, with Gerd's fingerprints on it, and four shots fired.

That was one more shot than Sal remembered having been fired at him on the yacht. As he was a practiced hand at retaining such details, the police, and we, accepted the accuracy of his recollection and assumed that the fourth shot had gone into Gerd, and rested somewhere at the bottom of the Mediterranean, along with what remained of Gerd, and of Skye's dreams.

SKYE ARRANGED a memorial service for him near the harbor, on that quiet solemn stretch of beach in front of Les Catamarans where Sal and I had lunched. It was a strangely gloomy day, the first that was overcast in my experience of Saint-Tropez. The clouds were thick, dark gray, and hanging very close to the hill peaks of Sainte-Maxime, across the water. The gulf itself was the color of slate, streaks of dismal mist coming down almost to its surface, as though all of nature were honoring Skye by joining in her melancholy.

Five straight-backed windsurfers clad in wet suits, shiny black against their sails, moved in a mourner's line across the still surface of the water. The colors of the sails were likewise muted, silvers and blues and whites and grays. Each sail flew a set of long black ribbons, which floated above the mast. The first of the surfers headed out toward the center of the gulf, his face like the carven figurehead on the prow of an ancient galleon, sailing fearless into eternity. Tied to his waist was a great black ribbon, connecting him at long, flexible distance with the surfer behind, who wore a like sash, banding him to

228

the one behind, and so on down the line to the fifth. So stately was their progress across the quiet water that the birds stood stationary attendance on the beach, as though they could not compete with such effortless grace.

Except for one. High above it all soared a solitary hawk, resting on a current of air. And I thought, maybe that's Gerd. Maybe he's finally learned to float, and see where it carries him.

I HAVE a lot of trouble with death. I know everybody does, but it seems, somehow, a little different for me because I am so convinced that this is not all we have, what we see here, that life is just part of it, and death a transition to some other segment of the journey. So, knowing that, I wonder why I weep.

I suppose it's because of what the one who dies might have missed, the pleasures he didn't enjoy, the food he didn't taste, the music he didn't hear, the kisses he didn't get, or, worse, return. But mostly I know I am weeping for myself, because of what I will miss now, the hole where that person used to be. I remember the words that the American Indians say, or said: "We have time and yet to spare, and I will meet you again at the end of the road." And I think, yes, of course, but what if not? And I always wish I had had the chance to say good-by.

One stepfather I really loved I said good-by to, and it made it all a lot easier. We hadn't spoken for nearly a year—I was shy about calling him. He wasn't married to my mother any-more, the girl he was married to was younger than I, and I always had the feeling she didn't enjoy how close we had been. But one morning, out of some curious need that turned out to be a dark intuition, I called him. We had a long, spirited talk, and when it was over I said, "I love you." And he said, "Thank you." And that afternoon he died.

So much of life you don't get a chance to finish off neatly. It just lies around, like a scarf, with its hem unraveled. I decided people should say "I love you" as often as they can. Because you never know when it's the last time you're going to see or talk to somebody, and if that's how it's ended, well, then you won't feel so awful when they're not there anymore. Of course, the trick is finding the people you can say "I love you" to, without feeling like a phony.

Also there are those who can't take affection, who feel suspicious if someone says "I love you" to them, since they're not sure they deserve it, and mistrust anyone who gives love too easily. So I suppose as a general rule, it's more circumspect not to say too much. But just in case that's it for either of you, it's wise to make a point of saying good-by.

Which means God be with you. Most of the people I know would find that just as hard to handle as "I love you." If that turns out to be the truth, then we have time and yet to spare, and we will meet again at the end of the road. I hope that's how it really is, and affirm to myself that's how it is. But in any event, it's a great conviction to have, because if I'm wrong, I'll never know.

WHEN THE surfers were all the way to the center of the gulf, black ribbons streaming from their sails and their waists, Skye moved a small canoe out into the water. In it was the portrait Gerd had done of her, and a lot of spilled gasoline. With a long lit pole she set it on fire and gave him a Viking funeral.

For the sake of symmetry and moral correctness I would like to say that no one but us was at the service, that of all those who knew him, or thought they did, no one came. But it was, in fact, the biggest event in Saint-Tropez since the opening of Byblos, with many of the very people present who had, I'm sure, been there, wearing what looked like the same clothes they wore to disco.

A little ways down the beach a woman unconnected with the official gathering, apparently unruffled by it, dunked her bare-bottomed baby in the water. His happy squeals echoed over the lakelike calm of the cove. Even in the midst of death, I was reminded, we are in the midst of life, except where they're siloing missiles.

There was no publicity about the real reason for Gerd's suicide. Sal was gentleman enough to keep the fact of Gerd's assistants, and the unlaudable origin of the paintings, to himself, as did the rest of us who knew. The general assumption was that Gerd had shot himself in grief over Charlotte's death, which most people who read her obituary could relate to, since the newspapers published, along with the facts, how much she had been worth.

There seemed no reason to make the art scandal public, since there were no survivors to benefit from the revelation. Nor had Gerd committed an actual crime, just because his art wasn't really art, and his talent wasn't. In fact, looking at the solemn, clouded canvas that was his memorial tribute, the wet-suited, black-ribboned surfers on that lugubrious horizon, trailing clouds of mourning, I could not help thinking that if his life had not been sufficiently artful, his death was, just as he had prophesized.

And as for his character, he could have killed Sal and he hadn't. Whatever his motivation was, it seemed to reinforce what Skye had maintained all along, that he wasn't a terrible

231

person. So I shed a tear or two or twenty for him, not because I hadn't said good-by, but because he and Skye hadn't had a chance to.

The little canoe, alight with orange and purple flames, rolled gently under the water and sizzled into silence. I put my arms around Skye. She put her arms around me. And Sal put his arms around both of us.

THE NEXT morning Sal and I lay in his room at Les Bergerettes, my head on his chest in that way I had come to know and love so well. I realized then I hadn't asked him the most basic question imperiling our relationship, determining what it was going to be, or if it was going to be anything anymore. I wanted to show great care about the manner in which I asked a question, having learned—I hoped—what annoyed him.

So "How long have your parents been married?" was what I said, my fingers gently curling around the soft hair on his chest, as my question did around my anxiety.

"Forty years," he said

"What a nice run. Are your brothers and sisters married?"

"My two sisters, yes. My brother's divorced." He kissed me. "What are you trying to ask?"

"Basic questions," I said. "Life questions." I struggled to sound casual. "After all, I don't know that much about you, except that you're a wonderful lover, and you're decent, and you make me happy."

"What else do you need to know?"

"Do you have any pets?"

"I've got a dog." He sighed once. "My wife got the cat."

"Your *wife* got the cat! Your *wife* got the cat!" I pounded my joy into his chest. "What wonderful news! Your *wife* got the cat!"

"You don't like cats?" he asked

"Oh, I don't mind them," I said, practically crying, "but I prefer dogs." I suppose right about then I would have gone all the way inside his skin and become a part of him if I could have, while retaining my own identity, if that would have been possible. And the two of us could have ridden the earth in tandem, as one, with him getting the saddle burns, which is my idea of the perfect man-woman relationship. "What about children?"

"What about them?"

"Do you like children?"

"Yes." It sounded a reluctant admission. "But I didn't want to have any until I was sure it would last like mom and pop."

"Mom and pop," I repeated with great affection. "Mom and pop. They must be so proud of you."

"Yes, they are," he said.

"Don't they want grandchildren?"

"I don't feel like getting married again," he said.

I could feel the joy go out of me. Not the sex, or the passion, but that which has roots in our real happiness, which I know comes only from giving, wanting nothing in return, only I'm not that enlightened.

"Not right away," he said, and moved on top of me.

"I understand," I said, sorrowful, but discerning, the way the wisest women have always been.

"So we'll have to wait a couple of weeks," he said, and kissed me. Then he was into every part of me accessible to him, plunging his tongue into my mouth while the rest of him did the rest of it, so there was no way I could shriek my happiness.

WHEN I went back to the villa I was oddly devastated for Skye. I felt torn up and disloyal, because it was all ending so happily for me, and sadly for her. Not that I am so foolish as to think there are unqualifiedly happy endings, but it is reassuring to know there are happy durings, one of which I was being gifted with.

But what of my beautiful, luminous companion? What would happen to her? Love that comes to a bouyant conclusion, for as long as it stays afloat, is like a reprieve from a bad dream, waking to find you haven't slept through the exam at all. How could I leave her to sink? How could I even share my jubilation? How could I ask her to rejoice with me when she was in mourning.

Oddly, her appearance was not in the least funereal. She had shed her dark clothes and appeared to have been out in the sun, which had risen again that morning, bright, transcendent. Her color was high, her skin that fabulous color that blondes get when they are actually brunettes. She was wearing a peach-colored shirt, soft cotton, clinging to her breasts, and sleeveless, so her arms showed in all their sparely rounded, lovely proportion; slightly muscular they looked, as though she'd swum a very hard sea. Hero paddling hard enough after Leander to develop interesting definition. Her shorts were the same pale peach color, ripe pastel against her tanned thighs, tight across her flat, long belly, pulling at her shapely behind. She looked bursting, as if she were not just dressed in peach color, but was herself an actual peach, ripe to popping, nearly coming out of not just her clothes but her skin.

She was running around her bedroom collecting things, putting them in Sportsac-y little zippered packages, vital things, they looked to me, like toothbrush and toothpaste and cologne. She hardly even stopped to focus on my return to the villa, or ask me why I looked so happy, in which case I would have had to try to conceal some measure of my bliss.

But it wasn't necessary. She seemed almost not to notice I was there. Or even care.

"What are you doing?" I said.

"Oh . . ." She was almost singing, half breathing, half sighing, covering the words with a sort of melody, as they came out. Her skin looked the color of hazelnuts, her eyes the bottom rung of the rainbow, blue bleeding into their gray, staining them lavender. The sun had streaked her blonded hair white around its edges so that her face looked like it was framed with the stuff that pillows around Christmas trees. "I thought maybe I'd go on a little trip. Clear my mind. You know."

I didn't know. It struck me as passing strange, even considering all she'd been through, that this perfect hostess, my best friend, would cut out and leave me there, all alone in a villa in the South of France, poor thing. Of course, she realized Sal was in the picture, but not in as deep as he was. So it was rather startling behavior. Giddy behavior. Not exactly that of someone who was sad. More someone absolutely floating.

Well, being as I was practically a private investigator through impending marriage, it didn't take me too long to figure it out . . . I watched her pack, paying particular attention to the beauty of the lingerie. And I thought, a man who could pretend to be the premier painter of his day could certainly pretend to be dead. Obviously it was easier faking suicide than genius. And it wasn't as if they had found a body, or now ever would . . .

"He's alive, isn't he?"

"Who?" she tried to say, as if she didn't know what I meant. But not being as practiced at deceit or even omission as anyone else involved in the tale, she wasn't very convincing.

235

"He'll throw you away," I said. "He'll use you up and throw you away." I wasn't really sure what I was saying was correct, but felt in the midst of all this brightness that someone should give a warning, one witch on the heath, just in case.

"I haven't the least idea what you're talking about," Skye said, closing her suitcase.

"What are you going to do with your life?" I asked her.

"Enjoy it," she said, and kissed me. And hugged me, while the houseman took her suitcases down to the car.

Then I was crying again. We both were. Because life is so provocative, churning up emotions like a Cuisinart, and we have to be so careful to disconnect the plug before we change the blades.

WELL, OBVIOUSLY, in my opinion anyway, he didn't deserve her. But he had enough appreciation of what she was to have said she should love someone who did deserve her, like herself. I suppose that's the best any of us can do, even if we're lucky enough to find someone who finally appreciates us, is have affection for ourselves, so we don't just puppy-dog through the universe looking for a pat. Smart as Gerd was, maybe he could practice what he wanted to preach. Now that he was dead (ha!) maybe he could be resurrected and come back as a better person. Perhaps he could help her love herself as much as she loved him, though I doubt he could be that self-effacing, even officially expired.

In any event I didn't tell Sal what I knew, or thought I knew. There are some things even those of us who are about to become one must keep covert. The only thing that needs to be completely aboveboard in this life is how you feel about someone, especially, as I noted, if you love them. As The Man said:

"Let the dead bury the dead." For what need had such a lively fellow as Sal to be chasing a phantom, when he could use that energy chasing me?

So we beat on, boats with the current, finally, borne ceaselessly into the present.